WE ARE SHADOWS

An Irish Ghost Story

GAIL GRANT PARK

Copyright © 2023 Gail Grant Park
All rights reserved.

This is a work of fiction. Names, characters, places, and incidents either are the production of the author's imagination or are used fictitiously.

No part of this book may be reproduced or used in any manner without written permission of the copyright owner except for the use of quotations in a book review.

For more information, address: leafrower@gmail.com

ISBN: 978-1-7379917-5-5 (paperback)
ISBN 978-1-7379917-6-2 (ebook)

Cover design by Patrick Knowles

To my husband, Richard, whose support and sacrifice have made this work possible. Thank you for encouraging me to create.

> "It is true, it is true, we are shadows cold and wan;
> And the fair and the brave
> whom we loved on earth are gone;
> But still thus even in death,
> So sweet the living breath
> Of the fields and the flowers
> in our youth we wander'd o'er,
> That ere, condemn'd, we go
> To freeze 'mid Hecla's snow,
> We would taste it a while,
> and think we live once more!"

—From "Oh, Ye Dead!" by Thomas Moore

PRONUNCIATION AND TRANSLATION GUIDE FOR NON-IRISH READERS

Book One

Taibhseoir = Tai-voar - a teller of ghost stories

Moira = Moy-ra

Deirdre = Deer-dra

Nuala = Noo-la

Seán = Shawn

Gallagher = Gal-a-her

Schull = Skull

Jeanie Mac = an expression of surprise

Press = cupboard

Boreen = country lane

Caoimhe = Co-eva

Garda pl. Gardaí = Irish law enforcement

Slán agat = Slawn a-gut (goodbye when you are leaving)

Slán abhaile = Slawn a-woll-ya = safe trip home

Taoiseach = Tee-shock, the title of the Prime Minister of Ireland, meaning "leader" or "chief."

Book Two

Stall the ball = wait, stop a moment (to stop someone from speaking)

Sláinte = slan-cha - health (to your health, or cheers)

Gobsmacked = amazed, surprised

Daithí = Dahee = David

An Gorta Mór = Irish phrase for the Hungry Times of the Irish Potato Famine Years.

Méabl = Maeve = Mave

Maimeó/Mamó = endearment for grandmother

Samhain = Saa-wn, (All Hallows Eve or Halloween in Ireland)

Book Three

Curragh = Flat, open plain of 5,000 acres of common land used for horse racing and training in the County of Kildare

Bang on = good, a good situation or person

Class = very good

Give it a lash = try it

Sound = good; excellent

Making a right haemes of it = messing up

Deadly = awesome

Go 'way = I don't believe it; that's amazing

Sleep of Foillen = Foillen, an officer of the household of the King of Leinster in Naas, feigned sleep so as not to meet with the visiting St. Patrick. He was cursed with the sleep of death instead, and never opened his eyes again. Inhabitants of the area remembered his fate long afterwards, and would curse an enemy with, "May his sleep be the sleep of Foillen in the Castle of Naas." (Life of St. Patrick, Apostle of Ireland, chap iii. Pp 66-67)

Leg it = hurry up; go fast

Griffith's Valuation = carried out between 1848 and 1864 to determine liability to pay the Poor rate (for the support of the poor and destitute within each Poor Law Union) - provides detailed information on where people lived in mid-nineteenth century Ireland and the property they possessed. See [Griffiths Valuation (nli.ie)](nli.ie)

Goon = fairly tame insult

Craic = (Krak) really good time, fun; or a greeting: "What's the craic?" = how are you?

Faffing = doing something without actually doing something

Gobshite = another tame insult

Fair play = congratulations, good job

Boot = trunk of the car

Yer wan = that girl

Jacks = toilet

Grand aul day = sunny and nice weather

Book Four

Niamh = Neev

'Get the messages' = doing errands, go shopping

'I will, yeah?' = I definitely will not be doing that

Barmbrack = fruity bread traditionally made during Samhain

Clannógach = clan-o-guh can mean luxuriant of hair, or cunning of nature

Cailín = ku-leen, girl

Cillin (plural cilliní) = Kill-een are historic burial sites in Ireland, primarily used for stillborn and unbaptized infants. These burial areas were also used for the deceased who were not allowed in consecrated churchyards, including the mentally disabled, suicides, beggars, executed criminals, and shipwreck victims

Chancer = someone who 'chances their arm', takes risks or pretends to be someone they're not, or tries to fool people into doing something; a risky character.

Gurrier = low-class, ill-mannered person

Langer = idiot, fool

'Away with the fairies' = crazy, in la-la land

Author's note on spelling

As this book takes place (mostly) in Ireland, and the main characters are Irish, I have made the decision to use the version of English that is standard there. Thus, you'll find colour but not color, recognise, but not recognize, etc. I would hope that my American readers can take on this challenge with the idea in mind that it is an exercise in learning a foreign language that doesn't need a subscription to Babbel or Rosetta Stone and will provide a feeling of accomplishment as you come to easily cruise over the unfamiliar spellings.

Book One
We Are Shadows
(IS SCÀTHANNA SINN)

Chapter One

Death leaves a heartache no one can heal; love leaves a memory no one can steal.

—From a headstone in Ireland

Schull, August 2009

As Moira picked her way through the cemetery, no breeze came off the bay to explain the now-familiar, sudden chill despite the stifling heat of the day.

Waiting for Deirdre to catch up, she stopped at an area free of headstones, where the tall grass was matted down, perhaps from some animal – an acceptable spot to enjoy the picnic their younger sister, Nuala, had prepared for them. She unfurled the lightweight quilt she carried, sank down with a sigh, and gave an involuntary shudder. She glanced back at Deirdre, carrying the picnic basket.

Their eyes locked as Deirdre's eyebrows raised in the unspoken question: *again?*

"I saw that," Deirdre said, as she plopped down next to her sister, her linen wrap culottes billowing out around her. "I thought you weren't working today."

"I'm not," Moira returned. "I have no clients at the moment, but I definitely just felt *something* …"

"Why pick a cemetery for our picnic spot then, if you weren't trying to reach someone?"

"I'm drawn to cemeteries. I'd rather come to this church ruin than one where I may run into a vicar. I love the peaceful atmosphere here—well, peaceful when I can't feel *them* reaching out to me," Moira said, as she took off her sun hat and fanned her face, loose curls falling from her messy bun and sticking to her neck.

"Have you seen anyone yet? Or just had the feeling?" Deirdre was always curious about the process Moira went through when communicating with …ghosts? The departed? Spectres? Spirits? She didn't know what to call them, so she just avoided being specific. She practised yoga and meditation, hoping that through being still, shamanic drumming, her special Blue Lotus dreaming tea, or any number of other hoops she jumped through, she'd finally get to meet a departed ancestor, but it hadn't happened yet. In some ways, she was a bit relieved. It just seemed to come so easily to Moira, who referred to these phantom visitors as the Others, as in Otherworldly.

At twenty-four and twenty-five, with only ten months between them, Moira, the middle child of three girls, and Deirdre the eldest, were Irish twins. They shared the same grey-green eyes and auburn hair, though Deirdre's tended more to strawberry blonde. They were also close in friendship, developed over the years as they often sided together against their younger sister, Nuala, who came along five years after Moira and garnered special attention as the baby.

Now, to appear a bit older, Nuala wore her chestnut waves in a soft pageboy. She was forever vying for her sisters' attention and dreamed of being a bigger part of their lives and pursuits. Her passion was cooking, which she indulged in regularly, helping out their mother, Dymphna Gallagher, at Sea Breeze Inn, the family business.

Deirdre remembered the day, ten years ago now, when she and Moira were teens walking home from school, and the conversation between them that transformed her from being a supportive and protective older sister, to a believer.

"Did you know Nana Brigid had two husbands?" Moira had said without preamble.

"What? No way. Where did you hear that?"

"Nana told me. She said Da reminded her of her

first husband, who died young because of his smoking and drinking."

Deirdre had stopped in the middle of the road. "Wait. What do you mean? Nana died a few years ago. When did she tell you? And why wasn't I in on that conversation?"

"She told me recently during one of her visits. Like Julia. Though it's been quite a while since I've seen Julia …" Moira had a faraway look in her eyes.

Deirdre's tone brought her back. "You mean it's real? You can actually see people who've died?" For Deirdre, believing that *Moira* believed in her visions had been enough. If they brought her comfort, what was the harm? But this, this was something else. She had overheard a conversation once between her parents about Da's more and more frequent visits to the pub. Ma had shouted, "You're just like Thomas O'Riley! You'll find yourself in an early grave and me a widow, like my ma, if you keep this up!" At the time, Deirdre was confused, as she knew Ma's ma was married, not a widow. Deirdre had never told anyone of this eavesdropped conversation, but now it all made sense with Moira's revelation.

"You believe me, don't you?" The shy glance Moira had given her had touched her deeply.

Deirdre had taken her sister's face in her hands, and looked into her eyes, searching for something there that would guide her next words. Then she'd smiled and said, "Of course I believe you. And I think it's amazing!"

Moira's body had relaxed and a broad smile lit up her face. Since then, they had not only been sisters and friends, but allies in this amazing adventure of receiving help and guidance from the world beyond.

~

"I received a letter from a young man in Tralee a few days ago," Moira began as she unpacked the poached chicken with Nuala's special red pepper mayonnaise, and the tabbouleh salad. "Just a minute—I have it here in my bag."

She handed the letter to her sister, and Deirdre began to read aloud:

August 4, 2009

Dear Ms. Gallagher,

I heard about you from my friend, Liam Brady, whom you helped a while back. I was hoping you might help me as well.

I was adopted as an infant. I never knew who my birth parents were until I got a letter from my birth mother, Eveleen, when I turned eighteen. It seems my mother was quite the beauty as a young lass. She had attracted the attention of a local landowner, a rich and powerful man named John McGuire, and before she knew it, found herself betrothed at the age of sixteen. But Eveleen didn't love him. She was in love with a young stable hand from the neighbouring village. They planned to elope, as her family was against that union and wouldn't give the required permission.

When her parents discovered Eveleen was pregnant, they sent her away to her uncle and aunt on the Western coast until she gave birth. Her family convinced her the best thing for me was to give me up. I was raised by the only family I've known, the Kennedys of Tralee, who were friends of her uncle. To further prevent the union, my biological father was encouraged, or persuaded to take a job in America. My mother never heard from him again. Her parents were relieved when the landowner was still willing to marry her despite her condition. He must have seemed like a godsend to her parents. They were unaware of his darker side.

Mother had left a letter with her uncle and aunt, and they carried out her wish to pass it on to me when I turned eighteen. In that letter she told me about my biological father and the circumstances of my adoption. She stressed that I not attempt to contact her, insisting that it wasn't safe. Then a month ago, I read in the newspaper that my birth mother and her husband were killed in an accident. Having never had children of their own, their estate is now being fought over by several distant relations.

A few days later, I received another letter from Eveleen, dated just before the accident. I will share her correspondence with you should you choose to take my case.

The Kennedys have also recently passed, and although I am still young (21 next month) I am optimistic about my future. Having this inheritance would be helpful, but for me it is more about righting the wrong that has been done to my family. McGuire and my grandparents prevented me from knowing my birth mother. She was afraid of him and her letters suggest that he may have harmed my father. I want it known what kind of a man John McGuire really was and that I am the son of Eveleen Hobhan and Jeremiah Quinn.

My mother's letters are not signed with her name or address; nothing to verify our relationship. Because of her secrecy and fear for her life and mine, I am reluctant to go through more conventional channels to pursue my claim. I have no way of knowing what the dangers are that my mother alluded to, and with her, my grandparents and the Kennedys gone now, I didn't know where I could turn for help. Then Liam explained *how you were able to get information for him from your more unconventional sources.*

Enclosed is the article about the McGuires' deaths for your information.

Sincerely

Seán Kennedy
(066) 9151988
Tralee, County Kerry, Eire

"Do you have the newspaper article with you as well?" Deirdre was already getting excited about a new adventure. She often partnered with her sister to help solve some of these intriguing cases. They'd even gone so far as to start a word-of-mouth business they called Gallagher Investigations.

Moira handed her a crumpled news clipping, or, as it turned out, a front-page headline:

MILLIONAIRE STUD FARM OWNER JOHN MCGUIRE AND WIFE DIE IN CAR CRASH; POTENTIAL HEIRS GATHER

The article said that the McGuires were returning home from an evening event when their Mercedes skidded on the wet roads and hit a tree. McGuire was pronounced dead at the scene, but Mrs. Eveleen McGuire was rushed to hospital where she survived on life support for several hours before also succumbing from multiple internal injuries.

"So, are you taking the case?" Deirdre inquired after she'd skimmed the details and handed it back to her sister.

"I haven't responded yet, but I think so … I'm already feeling like a few people are wanting me to," Moira said as she passed her sister a plate of the cold chicken and salad.

"Seán's mother?"

"No, not her yet. Though I'm hoping she makes an appearance. But the name 'Jeremiah' keeps coming into my thoughts. Since I don't know any other Jeremiahs, I'm thinking it's Seán's father."

"Can I help in any way? Any research you need done?" Deirdre worked as a law clerk in Dublin while she studied for her Bachelor of Civil Law with Irish at University College Dublin. It was summer break and she had come down to Schull to spend some time with her mother and Nuala. It had been hard on Dymphna for the past two years since the passing of her husband, Denis. Even with Nuala home to help her run things she occasionally slipped into a melancholy. It took the combined efforts of all three of her daughters to pull her out.

Moira was also enrolled at University College Dublin. She and Deirdre shared a flat not far from campus. With her interest in Irish history, Moira was studying Celtic

Civilization. She'd found it helpful when dealing with some of her more ancient visitors. She turned from staring out at the bay and focused on her sister's question.

"I don't know enough yet. You could look into this accident for me, if you'd like. And find out about the heirs that are coming out of the woodwork. How strong is their claim? How close is their relationship to John McGuire? Are there wills? That sort of thing."

"I'm on it. Well, as soon as we get back to Dublin, that is." The sisters were quiet for a while, each absorbed in their own thoughts; a companionable silence they were well used to by now. Then Deirdre turned to Moira and smiled, "This has sure been a great visit home, hasn't it? How do you feel Ma is doing? She seemed cheerful this morning, don't you think?"

"I do. You know she doesn't quite understand what goes on when I see the Others. But she does respect me when I tell her I've had a 'feeling' about something. She thinks I'm quite spiritual, or something to that effect. Anyway, I told her I felt Da was happy. I said I'd had a dream about him in which he'd visited me. There's no way she'd believe the truth, that himself was standing in my room not two weeks ago, and we were laughing together like old times. He was dressed in white and was very busy with various assignments, so couldn't talk long. He told me to tell Ma that he missed her and looked forward to when they would be together again. He said she was not to worry or miss him too much, because she had a lot of things left to do here first."

"And what did she say to that?"

Moira smiled. "She said that was very comforting and she wished she could see Da in her dreams as well some time."

"Well, that explains why I heard her singing this morning as she hung the bed sheets. She hasn't done that in … years it seems like."

"It *was* good to hear. I'd missed her singing … Hey, I need to stretch my legs. Want to walk along the cliff with me?" Moira invited.

"I'm pretty knackered after staying up late studying. I've got an exam on a summer reading assignment as soon as school starts. I'm going to stretch out here in the shade of this humongous monument to—'Hobart Murphy'—for a few minutes …"

Moira put on her sun hat. She hated her freckles and tried everything she could think of to minimise them. Her mother's voice came into her head then, scolding her with the words, 'a face without freckles is like a sky without stars!' She smiled as she scrambled over the rock wall and headed across the field towards the cliff edge.

Chapter Two

—

Ní gá eagla a bheith ar an ghaoth má tá do chruach féar ceangailte.

'There's no need to fear the wind if your haystacks are tied down.'

—Irish proverb

As Moira walked along the cliff edge, she sensed it first: a dark foreboding that began as an inkling in her brain but soon spread to her chest and limbs. By the time she could no longer move one foot in front of the other, a dark shapeless cloud had enveloped her and brought her to her knees. She tried to cry out, "Whaat—?" but no sound emerged. She was about to black out when she focused on the thought of Nana—her angel grandmother—and pushed a plea into the ether, "Please, help me!"

At once the blackness lifted and she found herself

on her back, staring up into the puffy white clouds of the warm August afternoon. As she slowly sat up, she felt a presence behind her, and turned. There was a shimmer of light at first, then an outline as her grandmother came into focus.

"Mamó! What *was* that? In all the times I've been visited by Others, I've never felt anything like that." Moira's heart was thumping in her chest as she took in deep breaths to calm herself.

"You've never been involved in anything that has drawn the attention of Dark Ones before," Brigid O'Brien explained.

"You mean Seán Kennedy's letter? What is so sinister about it?"

"Dark spirits on this side of the veil were often men of evil desires and deeds while living. Just as I, and the Others with whom you have connected, have freedom to assist our loved ones we left behind, these entities roam freely as well, unless curtailed by ..." Brigid hesitated a moment.

"By what? You must tell me! I never want to experience that again. How do I keep them away?"

"There are two options: You seem to have gotten yourself into something that has stirred up interest. You can let it go and back away from this case, or ..."

"Mamó, you know me. I can't walk away from

something I know I was called to do—help others in ways no one else can. What is option two?"

"You've already done it: called for help. I am here, and your other angels are not a few. And what we can't handle, there are heavenly hosts standing by to step in as well. Be careful, Moira, my dear. Not all your enemies will be from the Otherworld. There are dangers from several fronts you may be facing. I must go, but before I do—"

With arms raised high, she spoke with authority: "May the gates and doors and paths be opened between our worlds, and may the gates and doors and paths be closed to all those who would do us and our loved ones harm."

And then she was gone.

Chapter Three

---

*Is fearr a bheith i do bhó ar feadh nóiméid ná a
bheith marbh an chuid eile de do shaol.*

'It is better to be a coward for a minute than dead
the rest of your life.'

—Irish Proverb

"**D**eirdre!" Moira's voice carried across the field on a chill wind.

Deirdre sat up and looked around, trying to get her bearings after her brief nap. As Moira came closer, Deirdre saw that she was shaking.

"What's wrong? You look like you've seen a—oh! Come, sit here next to me. I've not seen you have this kind of reaction before." Deirdre frowned as she grabbed hold of Moira and pulled her down onto the blanket next to her. She wrapped her arm around her and said, "Tell me."

"It was horrible. A darkness that filled me with dread

and despair. I didn't hear or even see a person, only this cloud of evil; that's the only way to describe it." Moira sat on the quilt and hugged her knees to her chest. "But Nana B came and made it leave. She warned me that Seán's case may be more dangerous than anything I've—*we've*—encountered yet."

"Jeanie Mac, Moira! What will you do?" One glance from Moira and Deirdre rephrased her question, "Um … I mean, what's our next step? Did Nana have any suggestions?"

"She did not. I think we proceed as planned. If we're on the wrong track, we'll get some guidance, I'm sure. At least that's how things seem to work; we make an effort to figure things out for ourselves then help comes as we progress. Check into the McGuire's accident. Chase down the heirs. I'll take a trip over to Tralee and meet with Seán. I also want to meet with the relatives of Eveleen who took her in and arranged for the adoption, if at all possible." Moira stood up. Her shaking had stopped. The act of voicing a plan had given her strength and determination to move ahead.

~

"Moira! Wait for me! Ma said I could play at your house." Five-year-old Julia called out to her friend from her driveway

across the street, her blonde curls bobbing as she manoeuvred her new bike with her feet.

Moira found herself back in her five-year-old body, sitting on her bicycle in her parents' driveway, watching her best friend start across the street.

"I'm waiting for Deirdre to ride with me to the shop for a lolly. She's inside putting on her shoes. Can you go with us?"

Julia's reply was drowned out by the screech of brakes as the shiny black BMW came barrelling around the corner. Moira watched the familiar tableau of herself and Julia frozen in place, heads turned towards the sound.

At the moment of impact, Moira woke up with a shudder. No matter that this recurring dream was one she had memorised by now, it still caused her heart to race whenever she relived the last moments of her best friend's life. Those around her at the time wondered at her lack of apparent grief, going on as usual having pretend tea parties and outings with her friend, Julia.

Dymphna wanted to put her daughter in counselling. Moira could hear her parents arguing behind their closed bedroom door; it was hard to tune out.

"We should've let her go to the funeral, Denis. See? It's been over a month since Julia's death and she has again set out a place for Julia in her play tea party. She's not dealing well with the loss." Dymphna would belabour the point with her husband.

"She'll be okay. Give her time. Lots of kids have imaginary friends. I did when I was her age." Denis's attempts to soothe fell flat as he himself struggled to believe his own words.

"But was your imaginary friend your *dead* best friend, whom you saw run down with your own eyes?" With hands on hips and eyes blazing, his wife was too formidable an opponent for Denis to contend with.

"I'm going out for a smoke," was his non-answer, which was code for heading to the pub—the way he had dealt with most issues.

But why should she grieve when it had only been a moment after the accident before Moira had felt Julia standing beside her, both of them looking at Julia's bent and broken little body in the road? Moira had known instinctively that it was Julia, even though the spirit beside her appeared much older.

For a long time, it had only been Julia who visited, but as Moira got older and started to pepper Julia with questions (How had she grown up so fast? Where did she live now? Why did she always have to leave so suddenly? Why could no one else see her?) Moira's grandmother Brigid began to make appearances. Thus began Moira's schooling into the world of spirits.

As Moira lay safe and warm under her downy quilt that evening and contemplated all she'd learned thus far, she realized nothing had prepared her for yesterday's encounter with that evil presence on the cliff.

Chapter Four

—

Is fearr dornán scile ná dornán óir.
'A handful of skills is better than a bagful of gold.'
—Irish proverb

As her Mini Cooper sailed along the N22 the next morning, Moira's mind filled with thoughts of Seán and his mother. She was brought back to her surroundings by a blast from a motorist, alarmed that she was wandering too close to his lane. She considered herself to be a very conscientious driver, and berated herself for her lapse.

Somewhat shaken by the encounter, as she came upon the turnoff for Killarney, she was tempted to take a detour and clear her head a bit by Castle Ross on Lough Leane. She'd already been driving an hour and a half and could use the break. Memories of happy times picnicking on the castle grounds with her family and feeding the swans came back to her, but with still a half-hour to Seán's, and not knowing how long her visits would take, she didn't dare stop. She didn't want to be driving on unfamiliar roads after dark.

Seán's address took her a bit west of Tralee into Lohercannon, and as she pulled into the drive of the semi-detached, a young man was on the doorstep as if waiting for her.

"Moira, a'right?" He greeted as she got out of the Mini and came towards him.

"Good, yourself?" she replied. "Thanks for seeing me on such short notice."

"Well, it's me you're doing a favour." Seán waved her ahead of him, and she entered the tiny but neat front room. Its decor seemed a bit fussy and old fashioned for the home of such a young man.

"Do you live alone here?" Moira couldn't help but ask.

"Aye; the Kennedys were on in years when they adopted me, kinda set in their ways you might say. They've been gone some time now, but I guess I haven't gotten around to redecorating."

They passed through to the eat-in kitchen, but it looked more like an office than anything domestic. A computer was on the table and the small bookshelf in the corner seemed to contain mostly manuals of some kind.

"I work from home. I write code—here, sit down. I'm more comfortable back here than in the front room." He cleared off a chair of more books, and she sat. "Would you like a cuppa?"

"Oh, I'm fine; don't bother yourself."

"Are you sure?"

"Really, I don't need a thing."

"I have the water hot; I was about to get myself a cup, so it'd be no trouble."

"If you've already got the water hot, I wouldn't mind a cuppa; so long as it's no trouble."

Moira observed him as he got the tea from the press. He was fair and slight, but there was an air of confidence about his bearing that seemed to add to his stature. He sported a well-trimmed beard and moustache. Dark-framed glasses gave him a studious look, but his smile was open and welcoming. A mop of curly brown hair that matched the colour of his eye fell just below his ears.

"So, what more can I tell you?" he said as he poured the tea.

"Let's start with what prompted you to get in touch with me. Why not hire a solicitor?"

"I don't have a good feeling about all this with my mother's death. She was so cryptic before she died, not allowing me to see her at all. I'm so glad you are willing to help me. I have nothing concrete to go on, just an unease that there's more to this that needs to be uncovered. Eveleen's parents are both passed on now as well. I guess I'm seeking truth as well as justice."

Moira noted he used the more formal term for his biological mother, even referring to her given name instead of the usual "Ma," which was only fair, as he barely knew her. She wondered if he had anything of Eveleen's here in the cottage. It helped her sometimes to touch an artefact belonging to a person, to be able to connect with them.

As if in response to her unspoken question, Seán produced a thin packet of letters, tied with a string. "Here's the bit of correspondence from my 18th birthday when I got the first letter. The last I got about a week before the accident."

Moira reached for the packet, and as her fingers touched the paper, she felt an electric shock. She almost dropped the bundle, but was able to compose herself.

"Would it be okay if I kept these a while to look through them more thoroughly?"

"Of course. I have a few photos as well I thought you might like to have."

"Ah, sound." Moira tucked the packet into her satchel. "Also, are your mother's relatives still around for me to speak with—the ones who took her in when she delivered?"

"They are—the Brosnans in Dingle; about forty-five minutes' drive from here. I called them yesterday when you said you'd be coming out. I thought you'd like to see them if you have the time."

"Definitely. Thanks for arranging that."

"It's my mother's Uncle Rory and his wife, Claire. They are both in their seventies now, but still in pretty good shape. They weren't too keen to see you and talk about all this, but they are the only ones left of that generation. I guess they felt it was time to make peace with the past."

Chapter Five

—

Is fearr bothán biamhar ná caisleán gortach.
'A cabin with plenty of food is better than a hungry castle.'
—Irish proverb

Despite the tea and biscuits, when she reached Blennerville, Moira's stomach was telling her it was past lunchtime. With many tourists about, she was pleasantly surprised to find a vacant picnic table. As she ate her crisp sandwich and potato salad, she was oblivious to the picturesque sight before her. Instead, she focused on the packet of letters Seán had entrusted to her keeping. There were but three letters, their creases well-worn. She imagined Seán had read and re-read them many times.

The first letter Eveleen had left with Rory and Claire Brosnan to give to her son on his eighteenth birthday.

Moira read:

My dear boy, I love you already and you are not even born yet. I have felt you inside me these long months away from my home, my constant little companion, my one joy. I wish for you only good things, and that is why I must let you go. Please forgive me, and I pray that you won't think poorly of either me or your father; he was is a good man. We loved each other very much and had different plans for our lives together than what has transpired. When you read this, you will be old enough to make your own choices. Although I will most likely be living nearby, I beg you not to try to see me or contact me. My future husband is a dangerous man and I don't trust that you would be safe. He has 'taken care of' your father, Jeremiah Quinn, whom I thought had escaped his wrath by going to America. John has hinted to me that that was not his fate. I daren't inquire further into the matter but fear the worst.

You can trust your Great-uncle Rory and Aunt Claire. They are good people and will see to it that you receive this letter. Go to them if you are ever in need. I love you forever and always,

Your Mother.

Moira's heart ached for the distress and despair she felt in Eveleen's words. She whispered under her breath, *"Guide me to right this wrong to you and your son."* Then she packed up the letters and the remains of her lunch and headed back onto the N86. A half-hour later she arrived at the Brosnans' address.

As Moira pulled into the yard and saw the 200-year-old stone cottage, she thought of her own childhood visits to Nana Brigid's cottage in West Cork. The same grey stones taken from the land formed the house and barn, which was open to the sky. Stone lined the boreen in a neat retaining wall overlooking Coumeenole Beach below. And that garden! Only one lovingly tended could yield the abundance of roses, columbine, Sweet William, gillyflower, cowslip, and clove pink that greeted her eyes and filled her senses with their aromas. An older woman with pruning shears in hand was there to greet her. She was petite, yet wiry and strong-looking in her overalls, a stray lock of grey peeking out from under the wide brim of her straw hat.

"You must be Moira. Welcome to our humble home. I'm Claire Brosnan. I hope you had no trouble finding us."

"Not at all. It was a lovely drive and Seán provided good directions. What a beautiful spot this is."

"It is peaceful and quiet. We like it that way."

Moira thought she heard a slight edge to Claire's voice, as if she was giving a warning to Moira not to disturb that peace.

"Come in, come in. Rory is looking forward to meeting you as well."

As Moira entered the kitchen she was immediately confronted by a large man with a thick crop of snow-white hair. She held out her hand in greeting but Rory pulled her to him in a bear hug.

"Thank you for helping our Seán; although I don't know exactly what can be done, or even what he *wants* to be done."

Rory pulled out a chair for her around the trestle table where brown soda bread, homemade oat biscuits, and the most luscious raspberries Moira had ever seen had been laid out.

"Of course. Thanks for seeing me. What more can you tell me about Eveleen and the circumstances of Seán's adoption?"

Rory mopped his face with his hands and said, with more feeling than Moira expected, "Why did my sister have to be so stubborn and overbearing? Why did she make such a deal with the devil? Jeremiah may have been a poor sod, but he loved Eveleen. They would have given Seán a home full of love."

"We've been over this so many times, Rory; what's done is done. The Kennedys did fine by Seán. He had a good childhood. Better than if he'd been in that prison of a mansion poor Eveleen was in."

"Why do you say that? What was the situation at McGuire Stud Farm? Are you saying Eveleen was a prisoner there?"

"She may as well have been," Rory grumbled.

Over the next hour, Rory and Claire opened up to Moira about Eveleen's stay with them.

"John McGuire was handsome and charming on the outside. Eveleen was flattered by his attention, but when she ultimately rejected him, it was quite a bruise to his ego, I imagine. Eveleen was only sixteen and under her parents' authority. They favoured McGuire for what they thought he could give to their daughter and agreed to his plan to set Jeremiah up with a job in America. Basically, he bought them off. With friends in high places and the local gardaí in his pocket, there wasn't a lot the young couple could do.

"I'm not regretting for one minute that we did it…"

"Of course, it was good of you to take Eveleen in at such a time," Moira responded, encouraging him to continue.

"Oh, that, certainly. But I'm meaning the baptism," Rory looked at her side-eyed as if testing the waters with this bit of news.

"The baptism," Moira repeated, in a calm voice, though there was a fluttering inside her. *The baptism! Now this was some news she could use. A baptismal record would prove Seán's claim as Eveleen's child.* She maintained a neutral expression as if coaxing a skittish colt to come eat from her hand.

"Well, you see, the Kennedys *were* good people, God rest their souls." Here Rory crossed himself, "but … they were …"

"They were lapsed," Claire finished for him. "We couldn't be sure they'd be baptising Seán. So, my cousin, Father Lyons from a few parishes over, came the night of Seán's birth. Neither Seán nor Eveleen ever knew of it. Eveleen was exhausted and dead to the world that evening when Father Lyons arrived."

"And, is there a record of this baptism?" Moira held her breath.

"Sure, and we have it here in the trunk." Rory went over to a large dresser and opened the bottom drawer. Rifling through a pile of papers, he found what he was looking for at the bottom of a stack.

Chapter Six

Slí na nÉan

The Way of the Birds

Moira said her goodbyes at the door of the cottage. As she crossed the courtyard, the sharp trill of a linnet drew her up. Julia!

"Hello, my friend. I thought it might be you who guided me to this important document. Thank you. It will definitely come in handy. I miss you."

For Julia's fifth birthday her father had given her a set of binoculars and a bird-watching book. The two friends had spent hours in their gardens and neighbouring fields spying out the local bird community. They soon could identify various birds by sound as well as sight. Julia's favourite was the linnet, as her most requested bedtime story was Oscar Wilde's *The Devoted Friend*. Now the bird had become a special sign of Julia's presence.

Moira got in the Mini and laid the baptismal certificate on the seat beside her. She appreciated the trust that the Brosnans placed in her in allowing her to take the document. As witnesses to the ceremony, they both assured her they would be willing to attest to the veracity of the document in court, if needed. As she motored through the countryside on the two-and-a-half-hour drive home, she reviewed all she had learned:

First, John McGuire had visited Eveleen at the Brosnans' home shortly before she gave birth. His presence was menacing, even cowing Rory into leaving him alone with Eveleen. But Rory and Claire did not go far and were able to hear the raised voice issuing ultimatums: Eveleen was never to mention her child again; never to make contact. Her behaviour as his betrothed was unconscionable and he would not be humiliated by her affair coming to light. If it did, he would disown her and ruin her reputation. He had taken care of Jeremiah, so she needn't worry about contacting him either. There were more veiled threats concerning her parents' future well-being that struck fear in the Brosnans as well as in Eveleen.

Second, finding the baptismal record was huge. If the court accepted it as proof that Seán was Eveleen's son, he would be entitled to her estate, as her closest living relative.

As Moira contemplated these developments, she was oblivious to the heavy clouds gathering above her. It was coming on to evening and though there was little traffic, the darkened sky made it difficult to see the turns in the road ... and she was feeling a bit sleepy ...

~

"Wake up, Moira! Hit the brake!" Julia's voice shook Moira awake and she slammed on the brakes. The Mini came to a sliding stop on the now-wet tarmac, stopping inches from the stone barrier between the road and the river Lee. It was dark, with few cars on the road, but one stopped and the driver came to her window and asked if she needed help. Though she was shaking, she managed to assure him she was fine.

Heart pounding, Moira waited by the side of the road for several minutes trying to calm herself enough to continue. There was no doubt in her mind that Julia had just saved her life. Nothing so subtle as a linnet would do this time. She was now wide awake for the remaining hour of the drive. Operating on the pure adrenaline rush, she took stock and expressed her gratitude to be alive.

"Thank you again, dear friend," she whispered. "As much as I look forward to being with you, I'm not quite ready to leave this world behind."

~

The inn was dark as she tiptoed up to the room on the second floor that she and Deirdre shared on their visits home. It was after midnight, but Deirdre was awake and waiting for her.

"You're later than I expected. I assured Ma you'd wake her when you got in, so you'd better pop over before you get into all the details of your trip."

"I would have called," Moira said, "but by the time I got to a place where there was any reception, I was almost home and didn't want to take the time to pull over. I'll be right back." Moira, though overtired, was keyed up. She walked down the hall to Ma's room and eased open the door. "Ma, you awake?" she whispered, "I'm home safe. Go to sleep."

"Thanks, my love. G'night," Ma mumbled as she turned over onto her side before slipping back into sleep.

Back in their room, Deirdre apologised. "You must be exhausted with all that driving today. Don't worry about filling me in; we can talk tomorrow."

"It's okay, I'd have a hard time falling asleep anyway. Mind if I dump it all on you now?"

Two hours later they both fell into an exhausted sleep, but with a plan in place to ferret out the truth and right some wrongs of the past.

Chapter Seven

Is í an eagna an chíor a thugtar d'fhear tar éis
dó a chuid gruaige a chailleadh

'Wisdom is the comb given to a man after he has lost his hair.'

—Irish proverb

"Goodbye, Nuala; we'll be back at Christmas. Love you!" Deirdre and Moira both hugged their sister and turned to see Dymphna hurrying through the doorway of the inn carrying a basket.

"Don't forget your snacks." She handed over the goodies for the road, calling attention to the rather large jar of yellow-orange liquid with the homemade label: *Dymphna's Dynamite Fire Cider*.

"Ma, you know I won't take that stuff," Moira protested.

"Just in case. It's coming on cold and flu season and this will cure whatever ails you, so it will." Ma handed the jar to Deirdre for safe-keeping.

"Ma's right, this stuff is the real deal," Deirdre confirmed. As a teen, Deirdre had apprenticed herself to Ma with the ambition of becoming an herbalist like her mother and grandmother before her. By the time she'd left for university, she had quite an encyclopaedic knowledge of medicinal plants. She had created some of her own concoctions and tinctures that had given her quite a feeling of accomplishment. She was nowhere near as proficient as she hoped to be one day, but it was nice to be carrying on the family craft.

"Fine … Thanks, Ma," Moira said.

Deirdre and Moira got in the Mini and headed up to Dublin. The four-hour drive allotted them plenty of time for conversation and catching up.

"I've been able to spend a bit more time with Ma and Nuala this trip than you have. Ma seems to be doing better, but I'm worried about Nuala."

"Oh, yeah? What's going on?" Moira glanced over at her sister from her turn behind the wheel.

"You know she loves Ma, and the inn, and is grateful she's been able to be there for Ma these past two years with Da gone. But she'll be nineteen in a few months and has yet to go to uni or even get out of the hometown life she's been in forever. She feels guilty about wanting to leave

Ma at a time when business is beginning to pick up. She knows Ma needs her."

"She's always been our baby sister; it's hard to think of her as all grown up and wanting to take flight. But I can see her point. What did you say to her?"

"Nothing much; some sympathetic clucking, which was all she wanted—to have a sounding board for her frustrations. But get this—did you know she wants to go to culinary school and become a chef? She's enjoying the food prep for the inn. I know it's only breakfast and afternoon tea, but it's giving her an opportunity to shine. She's thinking her absence would only be temporary, then she'd be back and better equipped to help out."

"That's awesome; she'd be great at that. Remember how she'd always want us to play potions with her, making drinks and foods out of grass and seeds and flower petals from the garden? Even back as a wean she was in training for that career." Moira smiled at the memory.

"And she was always the one who wanted to help Ma make our birthday cakes and special meals each holiday," Deirdre added.

"What are you thinking? I can see the wheels turning. Have you an idea of how we can help Nuala?"

"Well, sort of. While you were out last night, I searched around for culinary schools. Did you know there is a top-notch school in Cork, only a couple hours from the inn? It's called Killacloyne Cookery School, and it's very reputable. There's a new 16-week course starting up in January. I was thinking I could take next term off and step in with Ma so Nuala could go."

"Wow, you have been busy. What's the cost? Have you said anything to Nuala about it?"

"Not yet. That's the thing. Tuition is €8,000 and another €100 a week for accommodations. Classes are Monday through Friday and with it being two hours away, that's too far for her to commute."

"I agree. But what if we checked with the O'Brien cousins in Cork? I seem to remember a few of them saying at Da's funeral, 'If there's anything we can do …'"

"You're right. That's perfect. Now that's settled, the next step will be coming up with the tuition."

"Hmm. Let me stew on that for a while. And I guess we should consult with Nuala before we plan out the rest of her life for her."

Deirdre laughed, "But we are so good at it!"

For the rest of the drive, they got back to work on the case. Deirdre would follow up with the law firm handling the McGuire estate. Through a contact in that office, she'd learned yesterday that no wills had turned up for either John McGuire or Eveleen. That was good news. According to the terms of the Succession Act, with no will, the estate would be divided up by a set formula. The McGuires had no children, which meant John's estate would all go to his wife upon his death. Eveleen died after him, so her assets would go to the child or children. As far as they knew, Seán was Eveleen's only child.

"Tell me again your plan for finding out what happened to Jeremiah," Deirdre prompted.

"Well, since we know Seán's father's name, and the approximate time he supposedly left Ireland for America, I'm going to search the Irish Newspaper Archives for any mention of violent crimes around the airport during the time of his departure, or any unidentified deaths. Eveleen's letters to Seán indicated the violent and vindictive character of her husband and even she feared John McGuire would harm Jeremiah. The fact that no one ever heard from him again seems suspicious to me."

"That sounds logical," Deirdre agreed.

"Then if that turns up nothing, we can start on the American side and check for a naturalization record, deaths, or even the white pages for him."

They arrived at their Meadowlark Apartment around two that afternoon. Moira dropped Deirdre off to air out the flat and unpack while she got a few things at Tesco.

When she returned to the Mini, arms loaded with

bags, she let out a shriek and dropped everything. The side window of the car was smashed in. The glove box was hanging open and Moira's heart sank. She rummaged through, taking everything out, though she already knew the truth: Seán's baptismal certificate was gone.

Chapter Eight

*"Then thrice around his neck his
arms he threw;
And thrice the flitting shadow slipp'd away,
Like wind or empty dreams that fly the day."*
—From Virgil's Aeneid

"The gardaí said there has been a rash of break-ins and car thefts lately." Moira filled Deirdre in as they put away the groceries. "And that I was lucky I didn't have anything 'of value' in the car, and that the car itself wasn't taken. I was so upset about the certificate that I didn't remember until they left that my laptop was on the floor behind the front seat. It's gone too. I'll have to go down to the station in the morning and make an amended report."

"I'm so sorry that's gone too. But the certificate! That was to be our best bet for proving Seán's claim." Deirdre seemed much more distraught by these latest events than Moira was.

"It will be fine. At first, I was devastated as well, but then I had a sudden inspiration—the parish register itself should also have an entry of the baptism. We would need to drive to St. Brendan's and have a look. The priest there should be able to give us a new certificate based on the entry, or we can photograph the entry itself. I should have done that with the certificate when I got it. I guess I didn't realise the threat we are up against, though I can't say I wasn't warned. I'm sure Claire's cousin, Father Lyons, was a conscientious recordkeeper and would have recorded the entry as soon as he returned from performing the ordinance. I'm glad I thought of getting the name of the parish from the Brosnans when I was there."

"When will you go? It's quite a drive and you had an awful experience last time you were out that way. Want me to make the trip?"

"That's okay. I'll head up in a couple days. Thanks, though. I want to check out the Newspaper Archives and if that doesn't pan out, get a start on the American angle. I'll call up at St. Brendan's first and check with the parish clerk to be sure they have the records. Sometimes they move them to the archdiocese. They might even be microfilmed by now." Moira was thinking and planning out loud.

"What do you think about a DNA search? I'm sure Seán would be willing to provide a sample," Deirdre suggested.

"But what would we compare it to? Eveleen was cremated. A comparison with the Brosnans would prove a relationship to them but not to Eveleen so it wouldn't be conclusive." Moira hated to dampen Deirdre's enthusiasm but it seemed a long shot.

"I don't know … maybe saliva from the envelopes of her letters to Seán?" Deirdre suggested.

"Let's see what happens with this course we're on. If it doesn't work, we'll consider our options."

"Okay, well, I'll head over to the law offices in the morning—it's too late in the day now, everyone will be gone—and check on the progress of the probate of the McGuire estate." Moira's calmness in the face of the break-in was already working its magic in soothing Deirdre as well. She switched gears and turned her attention to her rumbling stomach. "Want to order out tonight? I'm not up to cooking anything, even with all these great ingredients. I'm craving Freddie Rocket's Classic. If you'll call it in, I'll head over and pick it up."

Forty-five minutes later they were downing hamburgers and sweet potato fries, chocolate malts and coleslaw. The comfort food somewhat dulled the trauma of the theft, and Deirdre was entertaining Moira with her encounter at Rocket's.

"Seems they've hired an American to lend more authenticity to their American cuisine. I gave him a hard time when he called out our order for 'Dire-dree Gallager,' informing him that the second 'g' isn't pronounced. Forget about the slaughter of my given name."

"Well, at least you weren't named Caoimhe," Moira said with a grin.

"That's what I'm going to call my first daughter," laughed Deirdre.

~

"Can I drop you off at the garda station on my way to work?" Deirdre offered, holding out her second Vespa helmet.

"That would be grand; the bus is usually packed at this time of day." Moira gladly donned the helmet. "I can walk to the garage from there."

Once she finished reporting the theft of her computer at the garda station, Moira went next door to the Blackrock Library. As she didn't have her own computer, she figured she could use the internet there. She found a station in a quiet corner of one of the smaller study rooms and was soon accessing the online database of the Irish Newspaper Archives.

She focused on papers that reported the activities in and around the Dublin airport. With a birthdate of September 1988 for Seán, she calculated that the period beginning around May of that year through August would be the timeline when Eveleen would no longer be able to hide her pregnancy and Jeremiah would have left the country.

She pulled from the drawer the reel for the Evening Herald, July through December, and suddenly went cold all over. She felt a stupor of thought, completely forgetting why she was there and what she was trying to find. All she wanted to do was curl up in a ball and cry, forgetting the world and all its cruelties that seemed to crowd out any other thoughts. Although she remained upright, and to any would-be onlooker she would seem to be deep in concentration, her body felt like it was shutting down.

Struggling to make sense of what was happening, she thought of the time on the cliffside when she'd felt the presence of that menacing spirit. She attempted to cry out to her Nana Brigid for help, but her tongue wouldn't form any words. This was no imaginary danger; she felt in the clutches of something very real and extremely malevolent—a struggle for her very soul.

At the exact point when she felt she must give in and give up, she heard a sound, like that of a myriad of voices singing in multi-part harmony. The angelic choir—for that's the only thing it could be—grew louder, and as it did so, the malevolent hold on her weakened. As the one strengthened, the other diminished until she once again had control over her faculties.

She glanced around but saw no one. As she became more attuned to her surroundings, she could feel the reel of microfilm in her hands and was alert enough to go through the familiar motions of threading it through the spindles.

Still somewhat shaken by the experience, she did some deep breathing to calm her racing heart. It was then that she heard a gentle voice behind her say, "It's the first week of August you'll be looking for."

Although she could see no one, Moira felt no malice emanating from this presence, so she remained calm and spoke quietly.

"Who are you?"

"I'm Jeremiah," came the response.

"May I see you?"

A young man materialised next to her. He had dimples and a thick crop of black hair that fell to his collar and almost into his cornflower-blue eyes. He smiled at her, revealing a slight gap in his front teeth that somehow enhanced his features. She could see how he'd caught Eveleen's eye. She knew better than to reach out to him, but waited for him to speak again. His manner was shy but determined.

"Turn the crank, I'll tell you when to stop," he said, with a nod to the computer screen.

Moira turned it a few times until Jeremiah said, "Stop! There."

On the screen for the second of August was a brief story about a suspicious death near the Dublin Airport Hotel that had occurred on the evening of July thirty-first, a few days prior. The victim was not named and no perpetrators were mentioned.

"That's me. McGuire fixed me up with a job—an apprentice carpenter position, he said—in America. I didn't want to leave, but I felt I had no choice. McGuire had not only threatened me, but my family also, and of course Eveleen. Who could I turn to? He was tight with the law and had the means to do a lot of harm. I received a letter in the post with instructions that a room was paid in my name at the Airport Hotel the night before my early morning flight. The letter said I could pick up my ticket at the airport right before boarding. I got a mate to give me a ride to the hotel, and sure enough, there was a room reserved and pre-paid in my name.

"The flight was in the wee hours and the airport was a short walk, so I left the hotel before light. I hadn't gone far when I was yanked up by my hair and thrown against the brick wall behind me. There were two of 'em. I recognized one as a stable hand on the McGuire farm who had earlier threatened me and told me I would be leaving for America. The other didn't touch me, but watched from a distance. I couldn't see his face, but I thought it must be McGuire himself. I asked what they wanted, and offered my wallet, but the man holding me just laughed and said, 'It's me who has something for you.' I felt the knife go in … no pain, but his last words ringing in my ears: 'that will learn ye to take up with the boss's woman.'"

"I'm so sorry, Jeremiah. I'll do my best to help your son. Can you tell me what happened to … your body?"

"I got a decent burial in Glasnevin Cemetery yonder. I had no identification on me; the bloke who did me in took everything I had. There's a marker that says, 'unknown male age about 20 died July 31, 1988.' It's way over in a corner where they put folks who have no one to claim 'em."

"This information will provide some closure for Seán. He didn't say, but I'm sure he has always wondered if you made it out of the country or not; if you even knew that he existed."

"Oh, I know my son. I get to check in on him now

and then, but he's not like you. He doesn't know I'm there. I used to check on Eveleen too, and it would have killed me if I hadn't already been dead, to see her being mistreated by that monster. I know now he *was* the one standing off to the side when his man stuck me. But he's in a different place now. They keep bad 'uns like him in a place off by themselves, not where me and Eveleen are. I'm sorry she had such a horrible death, but we are together now, and we both want to help you help our son."

"Was that McGuire's presence I felt earlier? So dark and menacing?"

"Sure, and it was, but he won't be bothering you again. He's used up his chances for reform; he won't be let loose anymore."

Just then the door opened and a young woman came in to claim the other internet station. In that same instant, Jeremiah was gone, and Moira was left with the strange combination of elation and exhaustion that always seemed to accompany a visit from the Otherworld.

Chapter Nine

"When you get so near the dead, they seem more real than the living."
—Willa Cather, O Pioneers!

Moira printed out the story of Jeremiah's murder, then left the library. She still had some time before her car would be ready, so she stopped enroute at Blackrock Park. She found a quiet spot and removed her shoes, stretching out on the grass. She needed to take some time to regroup after her experience in the library and Deirdre had convinced her that earthing barefoot was the sure-fire remedy for any and all ills. She could hardly wait to meet up with Deirdre so she could share what she'd learned. Deirdre had left her a voicemail while she was in the library, saying she'd be home soon with news of her own.

Moira downed a protein bar, and drank some

water. Then, feeling somewhat refreshed, walked the two kilometres to the garage.

She made it home around half-three and found Deirdre in the kitchen peeling potatoes for their tea.

"What'd you find out? Do we have a will or not?" Moira wasted no time in getting to the point. She had a hard time with small talk.

"Fine, thanks, and how was your day?" Deirdre returned with a smile.

"Sorry. How was your day?"

"Complicated. Not only do we have a will, we have several wills." Deirdre set the paring knife on the cutting board and led Moira into the living room where they sat down. "I can't multi-task for this."

"Okay, shoot."

"It's a good thing I'm in good with my boss. Aiden asked what I was doing in the office when I was still on holiday, and I gave him a brief rundown on Seán's story. He offered some information that was extremely helpful. Even though our firm isn't handling the case, news travels in law circles. It seems John McGuire's niece and nephew, Tess and Tiernan McGuire, are twin children of his deceased brother, Malcolm.

"Yesterday they arrived at the office of John's lawyer with a will that was typewritten, giving them inheritance of the estate. It was supposedly signed by John, but the signature is suspect, and it was witnessed by a couple of the farm hands who cannot be located. Besides all that, it will for sure be thrown out, as it isn't handwritten. A handwritten, one-page note *was* found in John's desk, leaving all his assets to an assortment of his charitable foundations. Further investigation revealed the appointment at his lawyer's office to have it witnessed and notarized was scheduled for the day after the accident.

"The long and the short of it is that John McGuire died intestate. As Eveleen died after him, his assets would go to her designated heir. That certainly strengthens Seán's claim." Deirdre paused to catch her breath.

Moira jumped in. "Bang on! That is huge! Now for my breakthrough." As Moira began to recount her extraordinary visits from John McGuire and Jeremiah, Deirdre broke in.

"Slow down and back up a minute. You've just had a frightening experience. How are you feeling about that? Have you taken the time to process it all? You've got to be still pretty shaken."

"I'm fine. It was frightening, sure, but I'm glad it happened because I learned so much."

"Like what?"

"Well, let me continue and I'll tell you what I learned

from Jeremiah, not just about the case but about the whole world of spirits."

"Okay, but pause there a minute. I'm going to go brew us some tea—lemon balm, I think—that will help calm any latent anxiety and be soothing for both of us. My stomach is all in knots just thinking about what you have gone through."

Deirdre went to the kitchen and plucked a few lemon balm leaves from the plant on the windowsill. In a few minutes the water was hot and the leaves infusing. She returned and handed Moira a cup of the medicinal tea, settled in and instructed, "Now you may continue."

Moira smiled and took up her narrative. "Well, after the heavenly choir, (which was a confirmation of Nana Brigid's assurance that help would be available to me when needed, and it definitely was needed), I felt a more benign presence. I was pretty sure it was Jeremiah, because spirits don't just appear for the fun of it—they have to have a purpose for their visit—but when I asked him to identify himself, he did so."

Moira shared with Deirdre the details of her conversation with the departed Jeremiah, and added, "They're together now, Eveleen and Jeremiah, and they are both aware of and watching over their son. I also learned a bit more about the situation Eveleen was in at McGuire's.

I don't think Rory was exaggerating when he called it a prison. Here's the printout of the news article on the murder near the airport from July 1988," Moira said as she handed the paper to Deirdre. "Jeremiah confirmed he was the victim of homicide and told me where we could find his grave. John McGuire was definitely a bad one.

"This makes it all the more important that we get up to the parish and get that copy of Seán's baptismal record. Since I've got the Mini back, I can head up there tomorrow," Moira said.

"And you checked that it's there? There's no microfilmed copy available we could access via a library?"

"Correct."

"That's over a four-hour drive from here," Deirdre said. "I've been thinking—let's check with Nuala and see if she can get away in the next day or so. It's a shorter drive and you won't have to miss any classes so early in the term."

"I hate to involve her and take her away from Ma and the inn, but you may be right. I couldn't make the trip in one day. I'd have to stay overnight, and there's too many other things that I need to tend to here."

"Nuala will jump at the chance to get involved in one of our cases, even if it is peripheral. Sometimes it's hard for me to think of her as all grown up, but she is, you know." Deirdre said.

"You're right. I need to pay more attention to her. Sometimes her suggestions have been very helpful. I'll call her," Moira decided.

It didn't take much coaxing to get Nuala on board. Ma assured them she could survive a day on her own, and with Ma's support, the plan was put into place. Moira would call ahead and let the parish priest know Nuala was coming.

It was after ten when Moira checked that doors were locked for the night. She'd just turned on the tap for a drink of water when she heard a loud crash from the garden end of the flat.

Deirdre yelled from the bedroom, "What was that? You alright?"

"Checking…" Moira picked up her da's brolly from the stand in the hall. It was the one heirloom she had from him. She'd never had to use it as a weapon before, but it was reassuring to have it in her hands now. All was quiet in the living room. The curtains moved slightly from the breeze coming through a rather large hole in the window. Looking down, Moira saw a fist-sized rock on the carpet wrapped in a piece of paper. The broken glass reminded her of the broken window in her Mini. Perhaps that wasn't such a random break-in after all.

By now Deirdre was by her side. She reached down for the rock but Moira stopped her. "Wait! The gardaí may want it for evidence. I doubt there will be any fingerprints, but you never know the intelligence level of whom we are dealing with here."

"You're right. I'm calling the gardaí."

~

"No one seems to be lurking around the area, Miss Gallagher. I suggest you board up that window with some cardboard for the night and get it repaired as soon as possible." Garda Driscoll had arrived soon after Deirdre's call and now, a half-hour later, there was nothing much for him to do but go back to the station and file a report. "The note—does it mean anything to you?"

The page, torn from a legal pad, simply said, "mind your own business," in a blocky scrawl.

"I'm not sure. I have a client who is hopeful of inheriting quite a large estate. It is being contested. This could be connected. Do you think you could get any prints off the rock or paper?"

"I'll log it in with the report and follow up, but I'm not sure how big a priority it will be for the prints department."

"I understand. Thank you for coming out, Garda Driscoll."

He looked at Moira a bit longer than was comfortable. "Don't I know you from somewhere …? This morning! You were in the garda station. It was the car theft. I didn't take your statement, but I was at the desk at the time. Two incidents in such a short time bumps this up in priority."

"Thank you, Garda Driscoll."

"Good night, Miss." He nodded to Deirdre as she let him out the front door.

Chapter Ten

*"Help me to journey beyond the familiar and
into the unknown."*

—From the Prayer of Saint Brendan, the Navigator

"uala!" Moira sat bolt upright in bed, breathing heavily. Her cry brought Deirdre from the other bedroom.

"What is it? What's wrong?"

"It's okay. It was a dream. But a very lucid one." Moira's voice was still a bit shaky.

"Do you want to tell me about it?"

"I was playing chess with someone. Their black horse was threatening my castle."

"Their knight was attacking your rook," Deirdre corrected with a smile.

"Right. Anyway, suddenly I was *in* the game, not just playing it. I was standing in front of the castle, I mean rook, but it looked more like a church now. I tried to open the doors but they were locked. Then I was filled with panic and woke up seeing Nuala's face."

"What do you think it means?"

"I'm not sure, but I've only had vivid dreams like this a couple times before and they *did* mean something. I'm worried about Nuala going to the church alone."

"Seán's not that far away from Cloghane. Maybe he'd like to be in on the hunt for his baptismal record."

"Deirdre, you are always the voice of reason. I'll call him. As soon as it's light, that is …" Moira glanced at the bedside clock: 3:11 a.m. "Go back to bed. Sorry I disturbed you. But I guess I'm not sorry. Having a plan to call Seán has calmed me down a bit."

~

After hearing Moira's update, Seán was definitely in. He'd meet Nuala at St. Brendan's at noon. Father Feen, the current pastor at St. Brendan's, confirmed he would be home all day and looked forward to meeting Nuala and Seán. The church would be open and he would be happy to meet them there to show them the sacristy where the records were kept. They would be free to browse the registers at their leisure.

"I'll ring Nuala to warn her about my dream and tell her to watch for Seán." Moira frowned as the mobile rang and rang, then finally someone picked up, but it wasn't Nuala's voice.

"Hello?"

"Ma, is that you? Where's Nuala? Why are you answering her mobile?" Moira tried to disguise the rising panic in her voice so as not to worry Ma unnecessarily.

"Oh, she was in such a hurry this morning to head out on her errand that she ran off without her mobile. Can I take a message for her?"

"Ah, that's okay. Have her ring me when she gets in."

"I will. And how are you and Deirdre?"

"We're both fine, Ma. We'll try to get back down to see you soon."

"That'd be nice. Mind yourselves … love you, bye!"

"Well, I guess we wait it out now," Moira said as she disconnected. "Deirdre, if these two incidents—the car break in and the rock message—are connected, it's got to be about this case. What do we know about Tess and Tiernan McGuire? Could either of them be behind this?" They were finally sitting down to breakfast after all the arrangements had been made.

"Remember my telling you news travels fast in the world of law? That goes both ways. Listening ears in our firm could be connected to the group working with the McGuires. I wouldn't be surprised if someone knew about Seán and that we were working for him. I'll see what I can learn today at work."

Today was the first day back to classes for Moira; she would be tied up at least until after lunch. Deirdre's courses began next week; she was getting in a few extra days of full-time work at Callaghan, Cullen and Casey, Solicitors. They parted with plans to meet up for dinner at the Three Tern Tavern. It was a favourite, and not far from the Blackrock Garda station where Moira hoped to get an update before meeting Deirdre.

Moira found it hard to concentrate on the instructor as she kept checking her watch and envisioning Nuala's progress. Had she arrived in Cloghane? Did she meet up with Seán? Was the baptism recorded in the register? She sighed, and resigned herself to the wait, focusing on the instructor as he began comparing historic perspectives towards 'criminal lunacy vs. lunatic criminals.' *Ah, this could be helpful…*

Chapter Eleven

"From ghoulies and ghosties
and long-leggedy beasties
and things that go bump in the night,
dear Lord, deliver us!"

—Celtic Prayer

Nuala had taken the inn vehicle, Da's old pickup truck, so she drove a bit slower than Moira had in her Mini. She'd left earlier than necessary to compensate, and found herself at St. Brendan's Church in Cloghane at half-eleven. With a half-hour until Seán and Father Feen were due to meet up with her, she tried the church doors and was pleased to find them unlocked. She thought she might go in and light a candle for Da and say a little prayer; maybe one for Julia too.

Nuala paused to touch her fingers to the holy water at the entrance. She loved these old stone edifices that embodied her faith. Saint Brendan's was not so large that she felt lost in its vastness; it suggested a more personal communion with Deity. The vaulted ceiling sent her echoing footsteps up to the heavens. She lit two votive candles then slid into the front pew.

Nuala breathed in deeply of the old church smell—incense, damp stone, decay and … smoke? Had her newly lit candles put off that much of an odour? She shook off a feeling of unease and went back to her prayers.

Her devotions were interrupted by a rustling … mice?

Thunk! Definitely not mice. Running feet. Slammed door. Scraping. She froze in place. She saw no one, but the smell of smoke was much stronger now, and it was not coming from the candles. The fumes were beginning to make her throat itch. Nuala jumped to her feet and moved towards the front door. She grabbed the handle and pulled, but the door only jostled a fraction and remained locked.

Looking around wildly, she now saw the smoke coming from under a door to her right—the sacristy, where the records are kept! Panic started to boil up inside her as she stood frozen in indecision.

"HELP! FIRE!" she yelled, then through the ever-thickening haze noticed the side door. Holding her blouse up over her nose, she ran, only to find that way out locked as well. Her throat was starting to close up with the choking smoke and she croaked less loudly now, "*Help me!*" Then she heard it. Not with her ears, but inside her head she distinctly heard Da's voice,

"*Aw, come on, Nuala, don't be an eejit! Grab a candlestick off the altar and break through yon window by the door.*"

Stumbling-racing-coughing, she grabbed one of the two large metal candlesticks off the altar. She made it to the window and, turning her head away, swung with all her might. She heard the shouts outside at the same time as she heard the glass breaking. Gloved hands pulled away the shards and laid a blanket across the sill. She reached out and was pulled up and over into clean fresh air.

"Ah, lass, you gave us such a fright. Are you a'right?" A much younger Father Feen than she had envisioned was bending over her as she sat on the ground coughing.

"Think so … Someone there … the records …" A coughing fit seized her.

"Now, now, don't try to talk. Seán here saw someone running away as he came to the doors. A bicycle lock had been twined through the door handles. I met Seán as I was coming up the hill from the rectory. He was yelling for bolt cutters, but by then you had become very resourceful yourself and made your own escape."

Nuala looked up at the broken window and gasped

as she saw the coloured shards of stained glass around the gaping hole. Over the sill, what she had thought was a blanket was the priest's black coat.

"That was a stained-glass window ... of Saint Brendan! I can still see bits of a boat in his right hand ... I'm so sorry ..."

"Don't even worry yourself about it. We are glad you are safe and unharmed. You *are* unharmed? Whoever was in there didn't touch you?"

"I'm alright. I heard someone but didn't see them."

"It's too late to save the sacristy; we have no fire station close enough to make a difference. The room is stone and will burn itself out before reaching the rest of the building, but the roof will be gone as well, I'm afraid. Let's get you inside; we can assess the damage later."

Father Feen deferred to Seán to lend an arm to Nuala, and she was only too glad to lean upon this smiling young man with the soft, hazel eyes. She studied him surreptitiously as they made their way down to the rectory at the bottom of the hill. Facial hair made him seem older, but she guessed he was not too much older than herself. He had a boyish demeanour that belied the beard.

Father Feen had sprinted ahead of them and was waiting to let them in. "I'm afraid our nearest hospital is in Tralee, almost two hours away, but my housekeeper,

Anna, is trained in first aid. We'll let her take a look at you."

The housekeeper came in from the adjoining room. She was a spry looking woman of indeterminate age, with a halo of white hair coiled into a braid around her crown. She immediately took over from Seán and helped Nuala into a chair in the kitchen, then handed her a drink of cool water, which was exactly what she needed.

"Thank you, Anna. You're very kind. And …" Nuala turned and smiled at Seán, who was looking on silently by the door, "it's very nice to meet you, Seán. But I'm afraid your trip here was for nought, as I doubt we'll be able to salvage what you are looking for."

Before Seán could respond, Father Feen addressed her concern, "Now, now, say nothing until you hear more. It was your sister, Moira, I believe, who called me this morning. I wanted to be sure we had what you were looking for, so I checked myself." He went over to an oak, rolltop desk in the corner, took out a key from his pocket and opened the lid.

"I think you will find the entry in here. I felt prompted to remove this volume from the Sacristy this morning and bring it here to the house. I've learned never to ignore such promptings."

He handed Seán a slim volume, about the size of a student's copybook. Seán opened the marbled cover to the title page and read the handwritten script: "Births, Marriages, and Deaths in St. Brendan's Church, Castlegregory Parish, Diocese of Kerry. January 1986 through December 1988."

Seán stared down at the writing. His hands began to shake and he handed the book to Nuala.

"You find it. Please."

Nuala glanced up at him and something in her responded to the emotion in his voice. She felt a tightening in her chest and tears pricking the corners of her eyes. He looked so nervous and vulnerable after demonstrating such heroics moments before.

"When is your birthday," she asked softly, taking it from him.

"September fourteenth, 1988."

"Next week!"

"Ripe old age of twenty-one," Seán smiled briefly.

Nuala turned to the middle of the book then began scanning the entries. After a moment she exclaimed, "Here, shall I read it?"

Seán nodded; his eyes now closed as he swayed slightly.

"On this the fourteenth day of September, 1988, was baptised by me, James P. Lyons, priest at St. Brendan's, Seán Kennedy, natural son of Eveleen Hobhan and

Jeremiah Quinn, adopted by Dan Kennedy and Margaret Kennedy formerly O'Boyle. Born this same day at home and witnessed by his godparents, Rory Brosnan and Claire Brosnan formerly O'Malley, uncle and aunt to the child."

Rory's and Claire's signatures appeared below the entry.

Chapter Twelve

—

*"Here bring your wounded hearts, here tell
your anguish; Earth has no sorrow that
Heaven cannot heal."*

—Thomas Moore

"If I'd have realised the lengths these people would go to, I never would have sent you up there. Are you sure you are okay?" Moira was pacing the floor as she spoke with Nuala on her mobile.

"I'm okay. And Father Feen made out another certificate—I've got it here with me. Do you want me to send it registered post?"

"That would be grand, thanks. Nuala, I'm so sorry you had such an awful experience. I'd have you fax it, but the court requires original documents."

"Don't worry about it; I'm just glad we were successful after all."

"Right. Love you, bye."

"Love you, bye."

~

The probate hearing was scheduled for Tuesday, September twenty-second, more than a week away, so Moira, ever the optimist, was confident the document would arrive in time. Seán had applied as next-of-kin for a grant of administration, but without the documented proof, and as the McGuire twins had also applied, the matter had been bumped to the High Court for review.

Moira sat at her desk and got out every scrap of paper and note she'd made on the case. As she sorted through them, she wondered if there was anything else she could do. In the bottom of her satchel, she came across the letters from Eveleen to Seán. Now that the excitement of the past few days was over, she could look at them more methodically. She read the first one through then pulled out the second. It was short, reiterating the warning for Seán not to try to visit her. She took the third from its envelope and read:

Kildare, July 10, 2009

My dear boy,

My life here is almost untenable, though I won't

worry you with details. I feel like I am being held prisoner—my every move, my calendar, my friends (what few I have, and they are more of acquaintances) are closely monitored by my husband or one of his people. I'm able to mail this to you through a friendship I have secretly developed with one of the maids, Nellie Murphy. She is older than I and is from Waterford. She knew of my grandmother Mary. I trust her. If you ever desire to learn more of my life here, and my hopes and dreams for you, seek her out.

I saw your father last night. Jeremiah came to me in a dream. He seemed very happy and I wished to be with him. Perhaps one day, in a better world than this one, we can be a family as we had planned so long ago.

Love,

Your mother

Moira noted the postmark, dated a few days after the accident, was from Waterford. She wondered if Nellie (most likely, Ellen) Murphy had gone back home after the deaths of the McGuires. Eveleen's letter was dated a few days *before* the accident …

Her thoughts were interrupted by the doorbell. When she opened the door, Garda Driscoll was standing there holding out her laptop.

"Come in! Wherever did you find it?"

"It was brought in this morning, Miss. A lad found it in a skip behind the pub where he was working. Good on him for turning it in."

"Quality! Thanks a million for returning it."

As Moira reached out for the computer, Garda Driscoll first handed her a form. "If you would, please sign for it before I turn it over to you."

"Of course. Any news about those fingerprints?"

"Not yet, but the good news is, they are definitely on the 'to do' list. I'm sure we'll hear something in the next few days."

When Garda Driscoll left, Moira plugged in the laptop and was pleased to see that it was still operational. She ran diagnostics and malware detections and it seemed clean. *The thieves probably took this to hide the fact that they were really after the certificate; make it look like an ordinary break-in.*

She spent the rest of the afternoon looking for Ellen/Nellie Murphy. After about fifteen erroneous phone calls and ten left voice messages, she called it quits for the day.

~

It was Deirdre who woke first on the day of the hearing,

two hours earlier than usual. When Moira awoke, she found her sister outside on the garden patio doing sun salutations.

"Almost done. One ... hundred ... and ... eight! Just in time for the sunrise."

Moira had almost forgotten about this quarterly ritual of Deirdre's, performed at every solstice and equinox. "Autumnal equinox! I hope that is a good omen for the court hearing today."

Despite Moira's wishful thinking, the birth certificate had not arrived.

Nuala rang up, her frustration evident as she checked once again on its arrival. "I *knew* I should have driven it up there. The whole system is a joke! Useless! What time is the court hearing?"

"Not until half-three this afternoon. There's still time. The post doesn't arrive until noon. What does the tracking number say?" Moira continued to put a positive spin on it, but as she waited for Nuala to retrieve the information, a shadow of doubt began to creep in.

"'IN TRANSIT.' Not helpful at all. Moira, I think your optimism is misplaced this time. You're too trusting that everything will work out like you want it to."

"You may be right, but there's nothing we can do about it now. Deirdre said we can state what we know, that the evidence exists in the registers of St. Brendan's, and ask for a continuance if necessary."

"What does that mean—a continuance?"

"It means the court date will be postponed to give us time to get the paperwork we need for our case. And aye, I believe it *will* all work out, don't worry," Moira consoled. "One of the solicitors where Deirdre works is going to be there to assist us, pro bono."

Nuala was glad Moira couldn't see her eye-roll. Moira's "it will all work out" mantra would be more annoying if she wasn't so often justified. Nuala ended the call and decided to take matters into her own hands.

Chapter Thirteen

"Good friend for Jesus' sake forbeare, to dig the dust enclosed here.
Blessed be the man that spares these stones,
And cursed be he that moves my bones."

—Curse written on William Shakespeare's grave

It was a smaller turnout at the hearing than Moira had anticipated. Eight attendees sat before a large desk in a side room at the court building. A smaller desk to the left was for the court recorder. A young man and woman with a close resemblance to each other, in their mid-thirties, Moira guessed were Tess and Tiernan McGuire. Sitting next to them was their solicitor. Behind them were two men who looked like they would be more comfortable in overalls pitching hay than in court with white shirts and ties. On the opposite side of the room sat Moira, Deirdre, and their solicitor, Robert Casey. Moira kept turning in her chair to watch for Seán. The judge hadn't arrived yet, but there were still ten minutes to the appointed time, so she was, again, optimistic.

Moments later, Seán arrived, a bit breathless. He sat next to Moira, turned, and gave her a huge grin. She raised her eyebrows in question and he opened his briefcase. There on the top was a copy of his baptismal certificate.

"Nuala called me this morning. She told me the copy she'd had was lost in the mail somewhere. I didn't have enough time to go to Cloghane so I called Father Feen and he was gracious enough to bring me another copy. I legged it and here I am."

"Nuala. Bless her." Moira handed the paper to Robert Casey.

Another woman entered the room, looked around hesitantly, and then noticed Seán. She was rather plump and red-faced, in her late 60s, and spoke as she approached their group.

"Am I too late? Is this the group for Seán Kennedy?"

"I'm Seán Kennedy. Can I help you?"

"It's I who've come to help you, young man. My name is Nellie Murphy. I used to work for your mum, Eveleen. I heard the message on my telephone from Moira." Here she looked around at the group and her eyes fell upon Moira, who had stepped forward and put out her hand.

"I'm Moira, thank you so much for responding."

Nellie nodded and continued, "Eveleen was a good girl. So sad. A few months before the terrible accident that took her, I had a visit from my sister, Dora. Eveleen asked us if we would help her out. She had a paper she'd written up and asked Dora and I if we would be witnesses. We signed where she showed us, and then to my surprise, she gave me the paper and asked me to keep it safe for her. She said one day someone who knows her son may come asking for it. And that was you, Miss. I knew right away I had to come here when I learned of the questions around the McGuire estate."

Seán stepped forward, "My mother gave you something for me?"

Nellie handed a piece of paper to Seán, who read it and handed it to Moira. She read it and gave it to Robert Casey, saying, "You'll find that clinches the deal, Mr. Casey. It's Eveleen's handwritten, properly witnessed will, designating Seán Kennedy as her lawful heir."

Judge Flynn came into the room at that moment and all stood. The solicitors were asked to approach the bench. After what seemed like an interminable time wherein the judge reviewed the various papers put forth by the solicitors, looking up occasionally to stare over his glasses, he announced to the court, "Evidence supports

Seán Kennedy's claim. Case dismissed."

His gavel came down and there was a moment of stunned silence, but only a moment, for Tiernan McGuire jumped up and shouted, "This isn't the last of it!" and stormed out of the room, closely followed by Tess.

"We did it! *You* did it!" Seán turned and hugged Moira, who stiffened at the unexpectedly enthusiastic response, but Seán didn't seem to notice. Turning to Deirdre he said, "I haven't met you yet, but I'm guessing you're Deirdre, and I have you to thank also." He held out his hand for a more formal thank you, but Deirdre grabbed his hand and pulled him into a hug.

Robert Casey held out his hand indicating that was sufficient for him.

A surprise awaited them as they exited the room. The McGuires were still in the foyer, Tiernan in handcuffs with two gardaí escorting him out the door. Moira recognized Garda Driscoll and called out to him. He turned, said something to the other garda, who nodded and continued out with Tiernan. Garda Driscoll approached.

"As you can guess, the prints came back with a positive hit for Mr. McGuire here. Seems he's had a few run-ins with the law in his younger days that are now catching up with him. We have him for the car vandalism and theft, and the rock throwing. I'd love to pin the arson on him as well. Thanks for telling me about that incident, Miss Gallagher. Even though it happened outside our district, we'll be working with the gardai in Kerry to follow up."

~

A few days later, Seán was standing with Moira in front of a nondescript marker in a quiet corner of Glasnevin Cemetery. A brass plate on the headstone read: 'unknown male age about 20 died July 31, 1988.'

"Will you be wanting to move his body, perhaps to the McGuire Farm Cemetery when you take possession?" Moira asked gently.

"Maybe. Then he will be next to his love, Eveleen. I believe her ashes are buried there."

"It can be arranged at the same time as the exhumation to compare his DNA to yours," she added.

"I don't think I need to do that anymore. I don't know how you connected the dots to learn this was my father, but I believe you *do* know, and that is enough for me. I can feel it as I stand in this place. I'm at peace. Eveleen's acknowledgement of me as her son in her will, and the baptismal record is proof enough. We'll let him rest in peace."

"That's probably wise. I have a feeling that the two

of them are together now anyway, regardless of where their bones lie."

Chapter Fourteen

—

"May you experience each day as a sacred gift woven around the heart of wonder."
—John O'Donohue

Three months later, the sisters were all together with their mother at Sea Breeze Inn about to enjoy a quality Christmas feast, which Nuala had (mostly) prepared herself. Deirdre and Moira were finished with classes for the term. Seán was there as well, celebrating the completion of the case with them.

He stood up from the table and raised his glass:

"A toast! All's well that ends well. May your hearts be light and happy, may your smiles be big and wide. And may your pockets always have a coin or two inside."

"Cheers!" came the response.

Seán remained standing, and reaching into his pocket, pulled out a sealed envelope. "And to that end, concerning your pockets, that is —" He handed the envelope to Moira. "This, I hope, will be helpful in your future endeavours. It's not as much as I would like to give, as it will most likely be a year from now that we celebrate the actual completion of probate on the McGuire estate. These things move so slowly. But you have all done so much for me, I hope you will accept this token of my appreciation."

Moira took the envelope but didn't open it. "It was our pleasure. And we're so happy to have gotten to know you in the process, even if it was under difficult circumstances."

Later that evening, after Seán had gone home and the girls were alone sitting by a crackling fire, Moira pulled out the envelope.

"This is way too generous," Moira protested upon seeing the contents. She showed the cheque to her sisters.

"It's a reflection of his genuine appreciation," countered Deirdre.

"Oh, my!" was all that Nuala could get out.

"Well, this will certainly help towards tuition for Nuala's cooking school," Moira said. The sisters had discussed that opportunity together, Nuala expressing enthusiasm for their plans, with the exception of the financial aspect, which they hadn't quite resolved. She was amazed and grateful that Deirdre would put off her own graduation to give her this opportunity.

"Looking back on this little adventure, I have to say I am proud of you, Nuala, for being so pro-active in getting Seán's certificate. I also think it's awesome that you were able to keep your cool in that inferno and get yourself out of the church when you did," Moira said.

Nuala didn't respond right away. Then she said, hesitantly, "About that … It was the strangest thing …"

"What do you mean? You know you can tell us anything," Deirdre said.

"I so wanted to tell you, but I couldn't find the right words. I didn't want anyone to think I was a nutter." Nuala wiped away tears that started as she opened up to her sisters.

"Give it a lash, we're listening," Deirdre encouraged.

"It was Da! I swear! I was falling apart; I thought I was going to die. And I heard him, clear as if he were standing right there. He called me an 'eejit,' just like he used to; closest he ever came to saying he loved us." She chuckled. "That's how I knew for sure it was him. He told me to get the candlestick off the altar and break the window. So, I did."

She heaved a sigh and continued, "I feel so much better now! Is that what it's like for you, Moira? I was just so grateful for the help when it came."

"Exactly," Moira said. "And you're right, it's important

to always express gratitude and acknowledge the help when it comes. It will come more often that way. It keeps you humble, for sure."

"I get it. It was a bit disconcerting at first, but very cool. I felt peaceful and calm, and knew everything would be alright."

Moira turned to Deirdre and said, "I think we may have found another member of Team Gallagher Investigations, eh? Are you game, Nuala?" She put her hand out, palm flat down in front of her. Deirdre laid her hand on top and they both looked at Nuala. She grinned and placed her hand on top of theirs. "Team Gallagher!" They shouted in unison.

Book Two
We Are Roots and Branches

(Is fréamhacha agus craobhacha muid)

Chapter Fifteen

"In all of our ancient stories, water is the mysterious reservoir where the hero is to retrieve a treasure."

—Kari Hohne

May 2010, Dublin

Moira and Deirdre were sitting in companionable silence over their Guinness at the Braggin' Boy pub around the corner from their flat. The term had ended and Moira was officially a graduate. Deirdre, having spent the term down in Schull filling in for Nuala while she went to culinary school, still had one more term to go. They were finally reunited in their flat after the separation.

"I've missed you! It seems like forever since we've had an adventure together," Moira said.

"What do you want to do to celebrate your

graduation?" Deirdre asked.

"What do you think of a Grand Adventure?" Moira had a mischievous look in her eye.

"Like they used to do traveling the Continent?" Deirdre guessed, getting excited about the possibility of a long put off vacation.

"Well, I was thinking more like a transatlantic flight to the USA," Moira said.

"What? What are you thinking and why? I mean, I've always wanted to go to America, but what is driving this idea for you?" Deirdre pressed.

"I've had a dream—" Moira began.

"Stall the ball; let's finish up here and head home. This sounds like it's going to need some deep discussion in a quieter location, and with clearer heads." Deirdre grabbed her jumper from the back of her chair and stood.

"I'm so glad you're willing to talk about this. I'm serious—this is a trip of a lifetime." Moira flung her arm around her sister in a burst of enthusiasm.

"I didn't say I'm all in yet, but I am curious; let's go."

Back in their flat both sisters settled into their respective comfy chairs.

Deirdre spoke first. "You've had a dream … and?"

"I was in Caheragh, on the old family homestead, standing in front of the giant oak. There was a hole in the bottom of its trunk, and I could see water in it. By the tree were two rocks that, when fitted together, formed a type of breathing tube—like a straw—that I could breathe through when under the water. I picked them up and jumped feet first into the hole and the water closed around me. I descended through the water and landed, stepping out of a waterfall into a cavern.

"There were tunnels branching out of this cavernous room and one by one, I explored them. Within each was a room, entwined and nestled among the roots of the tree. Within each room was a person that I didn't know, but sensed were part of our extended family. Each had lost something and needed my help to find it. I woke up not being able to remember what any of them needed or how I helped them, but I had an urgent desire to go back and find out. I tried a dream re-entry, but each time, the water in the hole was dried up and I couldn't get through it."

"Do you think this is prophetic in some way? Or a foreshadowing?"

"I do. Water for me usually means a spiritual passage or journey of some kind; but I also think it could be an actual journey over water. And family members on a journey through water suggests America. We had many family members leave Ireland during the Famine Years, and as time has passed, we've lost touch with them, or I mean, their descendants. We've splintered and forgotten our own blood. This dream suggests to me that they are turning their hearts to us at the same time as I am turning to them. They need to connect with their family here as much as we need to connect with them."

"Are you proposing that we go to America and track them down? Where would we start?" Deirdre prodded for specifics.

"I was thinking we could start by checking with Ma for any old correspondence. Da's mum was the family historian and kept all that stuff; and now with Da gone as well, Ma has taken on that role. If anyone has it still, or knows where it is, it would be Ma."

"Sounds reasonable. I have some vacation days I can take at the law firm. Let's call ahead and ask Ma if she can check her attic treasure trove, then we can go down there this weekend." Moira's enthusiasm was contagious and Deirdre was beginning to get excited. Nuala was back at the inn with new confidence and credentials. There were no cases needing their immediate attention. It was perfect timing for an adventure.

Chapter Sixteen

"People will not look forward to posterity who never look backward to their ancestors."
—Edmund Burke

Moira, Deirdre and Nuala were gathered in the front room at the inn, waiting for their mother to join them. In honour of her sisters' visit, Nuala had made their favourite scones.

"Now here's something that might interest you," Dymphna said as she entered carrying a small suitcase. She set it down on the table in front of them and opened it with a flourish.

"Letters!" Moira, Deirdre and Nuala exclaimed in unison.

"This is all the correspondence Nana Niamh kept between her family in America and those they left behind here. But before you look through these, I think you should have a bit of a refresher course on your ancestors."

Dymphna paused. "I must say, I'm quite gobsmacked by you girls' sudden interest in the family history. I've been trying for years to get at least one of you interested in my little hobby, to no avail. What's changed to get the three of you showing interest in 'all those dry and dull names and dates' as you have so often said?"

Deirdre and Moira looked at one another, but it was Nuala who answered.

"Deirdre and Moira are going on a pilgrimage to find the lost Connolly relatives," she piped up.

"As I've heard, but why?" Dymphna's raised eyebrows indicated she knew when she was being bamboozled.

"Look, Ma," Moira said, "I've talked to you before about my intuitions and Visitors from Beyond, and you didn't seem to give it much credence. I don't want you to worry about us, but I have had one of my … *feelings* … that I need to undertake this journey. There are family connections there that we need to renew. We need them and they, I think, need us."

Dymphna's features softened. "About that … Nuala's told me a bit about your latest adventures. I can't deny that you have helped many people with your unorthodox ways, and as much as it is all still quite strange to me, I do believe you. I believe *in* you. And I want to help. Let me tell you about those folks who left us—" She pulled out a packet of letters and set them on the table. Underneath was a large piece of paper, folded twice. She opened it up to reveal a chart of family names with lines linking them to their parents and children.

"You may need to refer to this pedigree chart as I talk about them; we have to go back a few generations. Now, your father's mother—"

"Nana Niamh Gallagher," Nuala interrupted. "I've been learning about the family history from Ma."

"That's right. She was a Connolly. Her grandfather and four of his siblings remained in Ireland. They had four other siblings who emigrated to America over the course of about fifteen years."

"They left during the Great Famine, right?" Deirdre asked.

"An Gorta Mór hit the Connolly clan hard. The year 1847 was particularly bad. Poor Laws were enacted to try to give relief, but the majority of the costs to fund this relief was passed on to the landlords. Any tenant who paid less than four pounds a year in rent would have his share of the tax paid by the landlord. The Connollys fell into that category of renters and as a result, their family along with many, many others, were evicted from their homes by landlords trying to avoid these payments."

"Ma, that's horrible! Why did I not know these details of our family history before now?" Nuala wiped tears from her eyes with the sleeve of her blouse.

"It's not something we talked about much; the Hard Times were better left in the past."

"But where did they go when they lost their homes?" Moira asked.

"Extended family took them in. Younger kids were farmed out to relatives; the older ones—those in their teens—emigrated. It was a blessing that none ended up in a workhouse like so many other unfortunates."

"What were the names of the four siblings who emigrated?" Moira said.

"Here," Dymphna pointed to the chart. "There was Patrick, who left in 1868 when he was sixteen. Then Cornelius followed in 1872 and took his younger sister, Emma, with him. She was only fifteen at the time."

"But Ma, I thought the Great Hunger was over by 1852. Why were they still leaving?" Nuala wanted to know.

"The worst was over, but it was only a reprieve before there was another outbreak of crop failures in 1879. In the intervening years jobs were scarce; too many mouths to feed and so much death from disease made it hard to keep families together."

"Okay, you mentioned Patrick, Cornelius and Emma;

that's three of them ... and the last one?" Deirdre was trying to keep the narrative straight.

"Right, that was Thomas. He left in 1879. A few of the letters here are from Thomas, but most are from Emma; she was the family connector on that side of the water. They'd update the folks back home periodically as to who had married, who had babies that year, who had died."

"Did none of them ever return?" Moira asked.

"None. We've lost touch with most of their descendants over the years, which is a shame."

"I know. That's what's been bothering me. I'm feeling the need to re-connect. I want to go to America and find our cousins. I can almost *hear* their voices calling to me. Well, in my dreams I *have* heard them."

"So, the letters ..." Deirdre attempted to get them back on track.

"The letters," Dymphna echoed as she loosened the faded ribbon holding them together. "These are from Thomas and his wife, Nellie. Thomas spent several years away from his family hunting for gold in the Klondike during the Alaskan Gold Rush. Thomas's sister kept all the letters they wrote to the folks back here in Ireland." Dymphna pulled out one of the letters and handed it to Nuala to read.

Dear Sister,

I'm sorry I haven't written sooner, Nellie sent me some stamps but I lost them in a storm. We are 6,000 miles from home. I have eat more butter the last two weeks than I did 12 years. We've had bad conexions every where. We crossed the glacier at Yakatuk. There are 2 or 3 thousand persons there. The snow is awful hard on the eyes. I was snow blind for a day, but all our eyes are sore. The snow was 2 or 3 hundred feet deep and deeper perhaps. It was all uphill for 20 miles we had to pull up. We started at the foot of one hill with 150 pounds. Con and I thought we would never get to the top. We did not have a dry day this week. There is a good outlook at Yukon River, but if we don't find anything we might head for the Copper River or Dawson. I will try to write again,

Your brother, Thos. Connolly

"What a gruelling trip that must have been. It sounds like there were good prospects. Did they ever say they found gold?" Deirdre asked, poking through the various letters. Dymphna plucked one out of her hands. She had read them all so often, she almost knew them by heart.

"Here, read this one towards the end of their adventures. It paints a more despondent picture." She handed the letter to Nuala again, who read:

Dear Sister and family,

I was in Seattle for a time working as a labourer in a logging camp trying to get a few dollars but I have now been in Nome for some time. I feel very homesick and hate to go back without a few dollars so will stay here until fall. Does Nellie write to you? I haven't heard from anyone in some time. When last she wrote she told me Emma's husband Henry died. I don't believe they had any children. She must feel terrible.

How are my brothers doing? Are Ma and Da well?

There are lots of buildings going up here. A fishing cannery and lots of people coming in who need food and lodging. I was thinking it might be a good idea to open a boarding house or a restaurant as I can't seem to get enough gold to make it worthwhile. Give my love to all the family,

Your brother, Thos. Connolly

"It doesn't sound like he was very successful. Is there any more correspondence indicating he'd found anything?" Deirdre asked.

"Not that I know of. I've read through these letters many times over the years and I think they almost lost the farm several times, for not being able to pay the taxes on it," Dymphna said as she pulled out another letter. "This one has always been a bit intriguing to me though."

She again handed it to Nuala, who said, "This one is dated October 1902, which means he was there for a few years anyway.

"Let's see: *'My Dear Sister, I am in Seattle and will be heading East on the next train. I look forward to seeing my wife and children again. I have a little success, but not enough to stay here away from my family for any longer. I pray that you and my brothers and your families are all well. I will write again when I get back home. Your brother, Thos. Connolly.'*"

"I see what you mean. I wonder what he meant by 'a little success?' Do you think it was gold and he just didn't want to say?" Deirdre was excited at the possibilities.

"Well, if he did, you would think they wouldn't have had such a hard time holding on to the farm," Moira reasoned.

"Nellie sent a letter at Christmas that same year. Thomas came home in pretty bad shape. He'd lost a lot of weight and had 'a cold he couldn't shake.' He died in November, leaving Nellie with two little boys aged about five and eight."

"That's so sad. What became of them? Did they sell the farm?" Nuala envisioned those little boys and their mother homeless on the side of the road.

"I believe Nellie sold off most of the land and kept the house, living off the proceeds of the sale. Remember, there were several family members in the area that had come over and settled nearby. With family around, I'm sure they didn't suffer. Cornelius, or 'Con', lived several hours away in Western Massachusetts. He had quite a large family, but I'm sure he looked out for his sister-in-law. Patrick had died leaving a new bride but no children; I don't know what became of his wife. I'm sure she would have remarried."

"Do you know what happened to Thomas' and Nellie's boys?" Moira asked.

"I haven't a baldy notion, but I could do some research to find out." When the girls were little, Dymphna would often become so engrossed in genealogical research that it would be long into the afternoon before she would surface to realise her children hadn't had any lunch. Deirdre and Moira became quite self-reliant making their own meals and looking after Nuala.

"That would be great, Ma. And while you're at it, check for descendants of Cornelius and Emma as well?" Moira knew Ma would most likely do this anyway, but she had to ask.

Dymphna gave her the look and said, "I'll work on it. And now, I don't know what you have planned for the rest of the afternoon, but I've got tea to prepare for our guests." Dymphna, the innkeeper, emerged from her persona as she switched gears and closed up the trunk.

"Can we take the letters back to Dublin in the morning? I'd like to spend some time looking through them," Moira asked.

"You can make copies. I don't let the originals out of my keeping. Deirdre, why don't you take these into the office to copy. Nuala, you're with me in the kitchen, right?" She raised her eyebrows as she looked at her youngest, knowing how hard it was to tear her away from the company of her sisters on their infrequent times together.

"That's how we roll. Ta for now!"

Even though she was a member of Gallagher Investigations, Nuala wouldn't be joining them on this trip to America. It wasn't part of their business, as they weren't representing any client, but it felt like it was part of what they did together—help those who couldn't help themselves by utilising some unconventional methods, such as Nuala's passion and knack for dreamwork, Deirdre's many connections in the world of law and her general calming and practical influence, and, of course, Moira's ability to talk with the dead.

Chapter Seventeen

Spirits of my fathers and mothers, I call to you,
and welcome you to visit me.
Your blood runs in my veins,
your spirit is in my heart,
your memories are in my soul.
You are dead but never forgotten,
and you live on within me,
and within those who are yet to come.

—Irish prayer to the Ancestors

"Got a package from Ma. Think it's the results of her research?" Deirdre had been out for a jog and had picked up the post on her way in.

"Well, it's only been a few weeks, but sure, when she gets involved in genealogical research, she's unstoppable." Moira took the package and slit it open. Inside was a sheaf of computer print-outs along with a handwritten note, which she read aloud to Deirdre:

"Girls, here are the results of the last few days of digging. In summary, Thomas' and Nellie's oldest boy, Brian, married and stayed in the family home. From the 1900 census, it seems Nellie had a total of five children. I assume three must have died as infants before 1900. The younger son, Greg, never married that I could tell. Both registered for the draft in World War I but only Greg served. He died overseas during the war.

"I was able to follow Brian through to the 1930 census. His occupation was listed as 'agriculture.' Perhaps he continued the dairy farming business. In 1925 he was married to Isabelle Soucy. Their children were Philomene born in 1926, Virginia born in 1928, Ashley born in 1930 and James born in 1932. There's a James Connolly still living in Thomas' and Nellie's original home. I don't have any information about their children other than these birthdates, nor could I find a death date for Isabelle or Brian. I'll keep looking, though, and let you know what else I find. Slán, Ma."

"This is grand. I've got something to work with here. I need to have some quiet time and think on this; see if anything is drawing me in. What luck that there might still be a Connolly living from this line!" Moira was practically jumping up and down. "And with any luck, maybe someone from the Otherworld will also reach out to me if there is truly a need."

Also in the package were their favourite treats for the trip: cheese and onion Tayto crisps and Mikado biscuits.

"She does know they serve food on planes, right?" Moira said.

"Ah, she just wants us to have a taste of home seeing as we'll be so far away," Deirdre guessed. "But what's this at the very bottom of the box? Maps? There's a map for every conceivable location we might visit."

"I told Ma the other day when she asked if we had maps that our rental car comes with GPS, so not to worry," Moira explained. "She said we shouldn't trust our lives to something electronic. I guess she's taken the matter into her own hands."

~

"Moira, Nuala's on the phone; she wants to talk to you. She says your mobile is off."

Deirdre walked into the living room where Moira had the Connolly letters spread out on the table, and handed her the mobile.

"Hey, Sis," Moira greeted.

"Heya," Nuala replied, "Even though I'm not

accompanying you and Deirdre on your Grand Adventure, I have been seeding my dreams for any insights to contribute and —" she took a deep breath— "I may have seen something last night."

"Go on," Moira encouraged.

"A house. And a barn. I started walking towards the house, which I've never seen before, and something drew me instead to the barn. I walked into it and the space was dark, but there was a glow of light coming from a stall at the far end. I had to manoeuvre around bales of hay and tack and large holes in the floorboards, but as I got closer to the light, my way got easier. I reached the stall and saw a square cut into the floor, with an iron ring pull. Emanating from the cracks around the trap door was a light—the glow I had seen upon entering the barn. I started to pull on the ring, but then I woke up."

"That's it?" Moira tried not to let her voice reveal her disappointment.

"Well, not entirely. I was frustrated that I hadn't been able to see into the hole, so I immediately tried a dream re-entry, and it worked! You don't know what a breakthrough that is! I've been trying to do dream re-entries for ages but couldn't seem to get the knack. Anyway, I was in that liminal state, and this time I went right back to sleep and back into the dream."

Moira tried to be patient while Nuala paused for breath, but she rolled her eyes at Deirdre, who was sitting next to her listening in.

"And there it was—a box down in this hole and light was seeping out of *it!* It was too far down out of reach and there was no ladder. I was afraid if I dropped down, I wouldn't be able to get back up ... so, I didn't."

"You didn't," Moira echoed.

"I just woke myself up again. But my first thought upon waking was that this was Thomas's gold."

"Okay. Well, that's grand. Could you write down a description of the house? Or anything else you can remember?"

"Wait a minute," Deirdre interjected, "You are not going to believe this but I had a dream too. I wasn't going to say anything because dreaming isn't my forte, but I think we saw the same house. It must have been the Connolly home in Massachusetts, for why else would there be such a coincidence?"

"Now tell all." Moira was becoming excited; this could be what she was looking for in the way of direction for their path ahead.

"Right. I approached the house—a two-story, white farmhouse with a porch and green shutters—"

"That's the house I saw as well," Nuala interrupted.

"And I saw the barn to the left, but I didn't go towards it," Deirdre continued. "Instead, I went up to the porch and there was a man sitting there in a rocking chair; an old man, with a black lab lying at his feet. I introduced myself and he just said, 'you're too late. I can't pay the taxes and they are taking it away from me tomorrow.'"

Silence. Moira and Nuala were stunned.

"It can't be a coincidence, right?" Deirdre put into the space.

"No, definitely not. It sounds like that is our first stop, and perhaps we should move up our departure date," Moira declared.

Chapter Eighteen

*We speak to the Departed, through the veil,
the lines between worlds are thin and frail.
As the sun goes down, far to the west,
my ancestors watch over me as I rest.*

—From a Samhain Prayer for Children

June 6, 2010

"Maybe we should be taking a ship, like our ancestors did back in the day," Deirdre suggested as they packed.

"It's too late for that now, our flight leaves tomorrow. Besides, it wouldn't be the same; couldn't be the same. We'd have our own stateroom, whereas the old folks most likely sailed steerage. They called them 'coffin ships' for a reason. Although the motion-sickness might be the same," Moira said. They both had trouble with roller coasters and 3-D movies.

"That and the time it would take. It would have been a twelve-week journey back in the eighteen sixties and seventies. A cruise today would take two weeks, which time we can't afford. I'll go with the eight-hour flight, thanks," Moira said.

She was all about speed and efficiency, which made it all the more difficult for her to wait on Others to give her direction for this quest. It had been a few weeks since her initial dream that set her on this course, and besides Deirdre's and Nuala's twin dreams, she had yet to get any visits from those whose descendants she was hoping to reach. Yet, she knew from experience to continue to move forward with what information she had, and more would come, bit by bit. That knowledge helped to alleviate somewhat the stress of not knowing the full picture at once.

Now, as they finished with their preparations, Moira still felt a bit uneasy, not having a solid plan in place.

~

Their flight left at noon, and after eight hours in the air with only minor pockets of turbulence and one major episode that sloshed tea onto Moira's new jumper, they landed safely at Boston's Logan International Airport at three in the afternoon.

Even though Deirdre was older by almost a year, Moira was the one with more driving experience, so the rental car was in her name. When the agent saw her licence was from Ireland, he strongly encouraged her to get extra insurance, assuming it would be tricky for her to navigate the right-sided driving, and he was right.

It was after four by the time they got on the road and Boston rush hour traffic was in full swing. An additional glitch was that the rental car company was overbooked and they didn't have the car Deirdre had reserved. The smaller compact they were allotted was *not* equipped with GPS. Both girls could hear Ma's 'I told you so' ringing in their ears, and were grateful she had called them at the last minute to remind them to take the maps.

With Deirdre as navigator, they managed to get out of the city and headed in the right direction. Their plan was to take Highway 93 north, but they found themselves driving in an 'exit only' lane at the wrong moment and were forced to take the exit into Medford. Moira panicked and wanted to stop on the side of the road but Deirdre saw a sign for a hotel up ahead and coached Moira to the parking lot where they could regroup.

"I'm having forty thousand canaries right now; I just need to sit and catch my breath." Moira's hands shook as she released the wheel.

"You're doing grand! You got us here so far without an accident. I'm sure I couldn't have done that," Deirdre consoled. "Look, according to our time zone, it's about ten o'clock at night. I don't know about you, but I'm knackered. We have hotel reservations for tonight in Lowell, but I'm sure if we call them, it will be okay to delay our arrival by one night. Then we can give the map a good look and be sure of our plan."

"Alright, I just want to get out of this car, so let's do it."

After a shower and a meal in the hotel restaurant, both were feeling much better. Deirdre had called the hotel in Lowell and the kindly desk clerk ("Oh! I love your accent!") assured her that arriving tomorrow would be no problem. Deirdre pulled out the map of Massachusetts and traced the highlighted route that Ma had made for them to get from Boston to Pepperell, on the outskirts of which, somewhere, was the Connolly homestead. They had a rural route delivery number and hoped to be able to get a physical address from the local post office.

"I want to keep off these major highways and stick to the back roads, if possible," Moira decided. "It's too stressful with everyone driving full tilt."

"I agree. Looks like from here we can take 2A to 2 into … Oooh! Oooh! Concord! Look, it's even on the map—'Louisa May Alcott's Orchard House.' I absolutely adore *Little Women*! Remember when we would pretend that I was Jo and you were Beth and Nuala was Amy? We had to do away with Meg altogether, seeing as there were only three of us…" Deirdre was lost in remembering. "This *is* our vacation after all. And it's on the way, if we go this way."

"Of course, I remember. And even after 'Beth' died, I'd still come back and play with you, and bring Julia with me. You don't need to convince me. C'mon, 'Jo', let's get on the road again!"

Refreshed after a good night's sleep, Moira was more confident behind the wheel the next morning. They found the Alcott House without difficulty and enjoyed an hour wandering through the home and gardens that were not only the home of Louisa May Alcott but also the setting for *Little Women* and the place where it was written.

"It's awesome to think the Alcotts lived here at the same time our family lived right down the road," Deidre enthused.

"It is. Speaking of which, we'd better get going and check into our hotel before we try to find one of those family members." Moira gently pulled Deirdre away from 'Jo's Garden Plot' where she was scribbling down the names of the plants that were Jo's favourites.

"I'm going to plant these when we get a real house

where we can have a bit of garden to ourselves."

As they drove the less-travelled route from Concord to Lowell, the sisters were amazed and awed at the beauty of the countryside. It was almost as green as Ireland. Granted, these were different shades of green—darker and more forested with maple, oak and pines lining the road. The trees produced a tunnel effect of foliage overhead. At the approach of a small village or town, they could recognize the town centre by the 'village green'—a neat, fenced in, expanse of lawn, often with an accompanying bandstand or gazebo.

"Are you noticing these stone walls along the road?" Deirdre asked after they'd been driving for about a half-hour.

"They do remind me of home. Think of the man-hours it took to build them, stone by stone. No sheep in sight, though, like back home. I guess they were built for a different reason," Moira replied.

"I think they are amazing, and wonderful. I bet it was a bit of a welcomed sight for our ancestors, a glimpse of home. It's almost as magical a place as Eire."

Less than an hour later they checked into their hotel room in Lowell and found a quirky little place to eat lunch called Amber's Paradise Diner. It was housed in an old-time railroad car. They both ordered the special, a Boot

Hill Sandwich, which definitely satisfied.

Back on the road and headed to Pepperell, Moira was again questioning if she was on the right track. With no visitations forthcoming, she turned to Deirdre for guidance. "Do you have any insights that might help us know if we are doing the right thing here?"

"You're the one who's always telling me that no one is going to send a thunderclap when a still, small voice will do. The only thing I have to go on is intuition, but that has rarely led me wrong in the past. I sense that this is a bigger deal than just wanting to connect with family. I get the impression there are more people who will be affected by our visit than we realise. They will come. Be patient, they are waiting for just the right moment."

"But when is just the right moment, is what I want to know," Moira lamented. "I haven't seen or heard from Nana Brigid in donkey's years."

"Well, put it out of your mind for the moment—here's the Pepperell post office up ahead on your right."

∼

"Rural route addresses? Yup, we've still got a few of those for the outliers. Who are you looking for?" The clerk's name badge read 'Dillon O'Keefe.' Moira looked at the

Irish surname and took it as a lucky sign that they would be able to get the information they needed.

"James Connolly, RR 4, Pepperell."

"Connolly, Connolly, Connolly … Yup, here ya go. I don't have a house number, but he's on Kimball Road, to the very end."

Both girls looked blankly at him.

"Okay, continue on down the road here and over the covered bridge. Take a right on Hollis Road and go almost to the New Hampshire border. You'll see the Kimball Farm Stand on your left. Take that road and all the way to the end is the old Connolly Farm."

"Got it. Thanks a million. And can I get some international postcard stamps?" Deirdre handed Dillon the postcards she'd written at the hotel that morning, one to Ma and one to Nuala. She bought a book of ten stamps to keep Ma happy at least over the course of their trip.

They hadn't driven very long when they spotted it.

"That's it! That's the very house I saw in my dream!" Deirdre was fairly jumping out of her seat. "Oh, but there's no one sitting on the porch; and there's a dog, but it's not a black lab. It's more like the cockapoo that Cousin Ciara has …" She deflated.

"Don't worry, dreams are not so literal that you have to have every detail exact," Moira consoled. "I'm sure it's the right place."

As they pulled up to the house, a man, about the right age to be James, opened the front door. He stood watching them as they got out of the car. If the dog *had* been a Lab, or say, a Doberman or German Shepherd, they had the feeling it would greet them where they stood.

Deirdre raised her arm and called out, "Hello, I'm Deirdre Gallagher, and this is my sister, Moira. We're from Ireland and trying to find James Connolly."

"I'm James. Am I supposed to know you?"

"Well, no, probably not. We're your family from Cork. At least, we share the same ancestors from Cork, if you are James, son of Brian and Isabelle?"

"You seem to know a lot about me … What do you want?"

"We want to talk to you. Get to know you. And tell you about us. You know, a bit of a family reunion?" Moira smiled, hoping to break the tension.

"Seems like you've come a long way; might as well set a spell." James turned and walked back into the house. Moira and Deirdre looked at each other, shrugged, then walked up the porch steps and followed James and the cockapoo into the house.

"Have a seat; you want some water? Soda? I don't have much else to offer ya."

"Water would be grand," answered Moira, and Deirdre nodded.

"Grand ... you sure sound like you're from the Old Country. So, how are we related?" James returned with water glasses and a plate of Oreo cookies.

Deirdre pulled out the family tree charts that Dymphna had created and for the next hour, the three of them pored over the names and dates which no longer seemed dry and dull. They'd also brought current photos of their family—aunts, uncles, cousins—and some ancestral photographs taken as far back as right before the siblings all left Ireland.

"Well, I'll be damned! Pardon my French, ladies," James exclaimed. "And here I was thinking I was all alone in the world. That's a whole lot of relatives!"

"What do you mean you're alone? No wife or children?"

"My wife, rest her soul, died ten years ago of the cancer. We had two daughters, but they married and moved away. They have busy lives, families ..." Then he brightened, "I have a grandson—Alex. He's a young man now, in college. He stopped to see me before he returned to college last year. Oh, and three granddaughters. Last I saw them all was, let's see, a couple years ago?"

"Didn't you have sisters? And what of cousins? Uncles?" Deirdre persisted.

"Ah, yes. My sisters—Mena, Ginny and Ash—all

gone. Never got too close to their families. Husbands … not the warmest bunch." He smirked.

"That's so sad!" Moira exclaimed. "Did you not keep up with the Connolly branch of the family who settled in Western Massachusetts? Pittsfield, wasn't it?" Moira had done her homework reviewing Ma's research.

"Those s.o.b.s! No, no, we are *not* in touch. Haven't connected with those Connollys for quite a few generations now. After the things they said about Nana Nellie …" James became red in the face, jumped up and began pacing the room.

"James, I'm so sorry; I didn't mean to upset you. We had no idea what happened between your families." Deirdre stopped there, hoping James would fill in the details for them. She didn't have to wait long. James sat down and rubbed his face, trying to get composure.

"Grandad Thomas and Uncle Con went to the Klondike together in 1896. They were there two years, then went back in 1899 for three more years, but by then the Gold Rush was pretty much over. For part of the time, Thomas tried the Nome area when gold was discovered there as well, while Con stayed in Dawson. But by the time Grandad got back home in November of 1902, he was a broken man. The hardships had taken their toll and he was dead before Christmas. Uncle Con and he had made a pact to work together and share everything. Con got home a few weeks after Thomas, and came to see Grandad, but Thomas was too ill to see him, or when he did, he wasn't able to talk much. Dad was about eight years old at the time and said he remembers Con's visit. Con had yelled at his brother, demanding to know what he had done with the gold, what had happened to their Nome claim.

"When Grandad died, Uncle Con started badgering Nana Nellie. He was convinced he was being robbed of his share of the gold, but Nana kept telling him she couldn't give him what she didn't have. Terrible things were said on both sides, and the families haven't spoken to each other ever since."

After James stopped speaking, the three sat there a moment without comment. He seemed exhausted by the telling of his story. Moira's brain was on fire with conjecture as to what this news meant for her purpose. *Am I to be the catalyst to bring these feuding families together? Would any of the parties from the Otherworld intervene? This had to be a huge misunderstanding compounded by pride over the years.*

Deirdre reached out and put her hand on his knee. "Is there anything we can do for you? Are you okay here on your own?" she said.

"Aye, I'm 'grand,' as you say. It won't matter for much longer anyway. I couldn't pay the tax bill again this year.

The town says I have to tear down the barn because it is a hazard after the big storm last winter that collapsed the back end of it. Don't have the money to repair it or take it down."

"Where will you go if you lose the house?" Moira inquired.

"Don't know. I called my daughters and left messages about maybe going to stay with one of them but I haven't heard back yet. I'm sure they're discussing it with their husbands. I got on the list for the new low-income apartments in Lowell. I'm hoping my Social Security will cover the rent there, but I know there is a long waiting list. And I couldn't take Doodles with me ..." he stroked the little dog that had jumped into his lap upon hearing its name.

He continued, "I'm sorry ... I'm feeling a bit tired. Can we visit again another time?"

"Of course. We're staying in Lowell for a bit. Could we come back tomorrow to see you?" Moira was hoping to hear more about the Cornelius branch of the family.

"I just love old barns!" Deirdre interjected. "It doesn't look dangerous ..."

"Nah, it's not bad. The roof is caved in on the back corner, is all. Used to house a couple horses and the hay for the cattle, but that was long ago. Hey! I have some things I could show you if you do come tomorrow. Some pictures of the family and some letters."

"We'll be here!"

~

As they drove away, Moira turned to Deirdre and said, "'I just love old barns?' Not very subtle, eh?"

"Yeah, I was desperate. I so want to see if Nuala's dream of the hidden cache has any validity. And to think the authorities want it torn down. This may be the only chance we have to look, the reason why we are here at this place at this time."

There was no arguing with that.

~

On the way back to the hotel they took a quick detour at a sign that said, Trembull Ice Cream. It was close enough to supper and it appeared the shop served a lot more than ice cream. Its popularity was attested to by the packed parking lot, but with a dozen service windows, the wait wasn't too long. Moira got their famous lobster roll, and Deirdre ordered fish and chips. With a mini-fridge and microwave in their hotel room, they opted to take home half and leave room for dessert.

"Ooh! Grapenuts ice cream! I love Grapenuts cereal. What a grand idea to put it in ice cream." Deirdre chose that for her cone, and Moira went with a Caramel Cashew Chip.

"What does it taste like?" Moira asked about Deirdre's choice.

"Delicious; like little rocks in vanilla ice cream," Deirdre replied with just a touch of sarcasm. The regular size was so huge they wished they could take home half of that as well, but they managed to down all of it as they sat on the deck and watched families floating the Bumper Boat Pond at the back of the restaurant.

"This is feeling like an actual vacation, with the bonus of maybe solving a family mystery," Deirdre said, as she crunched the last of her cone and stood up. They had been discussing their visit with James and speculating on the possibility of finding Nuala's—aka Thomas'—cache of gold at the end of it all.

"It *is* nice to get away and to follow this path wherever it leads. I'm going to need some quiet time when we get back to the hotel, to see if I can tune in to any potential Visitors. If no one else, I could use a consult with Nana Brigid." Moira linked arms with her sister as they walked back to their rental car.

Chapter Nineteen

"All of us are in danger of dying; some of us more than others."
—Alan Bradley, The Golden Tresses of the Dead

An ocean away, Nuala found herself in a dream that she instinctively knew was not her own. She saw a young woman, about her own age, sleeping under a cherry tree. Then, *she* was the young woman, dreaming a moon voyage. A full moon shone a path of light across water. A boat was waiting for her and she got in. There were no paddles or oars, but as soon as she settled in, the boat began to move, as if powered by a golden rope that pulled her along the path of the moon glow. At the horizon line, the boat didn't stop but began to rise, up towards the light.

It should have been such a long voyage, but within moments they had docked at a wharf on the moon. She stood and placed a tentative foot on the moon's surface. It was a powdery grey that shimmered and sparkled as her footprint displaced the dust. She followed other footprints around a stone outcropping to a quaint café. Inside there were three older women sitting at a table set for four. It was all a bit disconcerting until Nuala recognized Nana Brigid as one of the three. Then she relaxed and enjoyed the ride.

Nana Brigid beckoned to her to sit with them and greeted her by the name of 'Katie.'

"Welcome to the Moon Café, Katie. We are delighted that you have found your way here. My name is Brigid, and though you don't know me, I am a part of your family and am well acquainted with your Nana Méabl and Nana Nora here with me. You are here to learn from the counsel of your Wise Women. Are you ready? Sip your moon tea and listen carefully."

Méabl spoke next, "My dear granddaughter, your music wants to be heard. It is trying to push through you every moment of every day. Don't fear it. If you don't let it out, it will find a receptive outlet in someone else. Seek solitude—openness, patience, receptivity—in the quiet you will hear. Be patient with yourself and listen to the voice of your soul."

Next, Nora spoke. "Dear child, music is unique to humans. It is a divine language. The song of the heart is a prayer to God. Sing every day. Sing loud and with all your soul's feelings. Then, when you are done singing, dance! Then, once you feel safe in your own soul-sound, you are called to share it with others. You are a gifted teacher and will touch the lives of many."

Brigid said, "Use the power of your music to heal yourself and touch the lives of others in uplifting ways. When you are authentic, you are true to the truth that is unique to you. Expect a Benevolent Force to assist you. Let its power flow through you and thus to the world. Trust that you have partners in the Universe that are helping you—co-creators with the Divine. Any act of creating, whether it be painting, writing, singing, or mathematics, is a spiritual covenant between the maker and these Higher Powers of the Universe."

Méabl spoke up next. "My dear Katie, unconditional love fuels the creative process. Love yourself. He has given you these gifts and wants you to develop them. As you do, you will have a greater capacity to give love and receive love in return."

Nora said, "We are always with you. We love you. We asked to be your ministering spirits, and we are glad that you have been able to recognize us as such. Most people are never aware of the great love their departed ancestors have for them. We were born generations apart, but you have touched my life in profound and eternal ways. I am honoured to have this calling to guide and inspire and encourage you to be what you have the potential to be: a glorious, celestial being, full of light and truth and love."

Brigid spoke as she stood up. "Now, it is time to send you on your way. And I promise that the way will be opened to you. Your destiny is entwined with a dear one of my own who is also reaching out to help you; she is called Moira."

Then Méabl and Nora also stood, and the three women circled around her chair and laid their hands upon her head. Nora, although not the spokesperson as Brigid seemed to be, did appear to hold some kind of elder authority, and was voice for the blessing pronounced upon her. With words that were unutterable, she conveyed the love and support, strength and abilities that were Katie's divine right.

They didn't escort her to her boat but watched her go with smiles and nods. The journey home was luxuriously slow, giving her time to contemplate and internalise all that she had seen and heard and felt. She awoke under the tree, now with the sun lowering in the sky.

Nuala felt herself separate from Katie and once again look down at her as if from above. Katie stood, smiling, and then Nuala woke up.

Chapter Twenty

"Only in fully releasing the desire for things to be different than they are, do we actually make space for change to occur."

—Aine Divine

As she pulled on her cardigan, Moira called out to Deirdre who was in the bathroom. "There's a lovely little park across the street from the hotel I noticed on our way out yesterday. I'm taking a walk there this morning before we head back to Pepperell. I won't be long. Catch you back here in about an hour for breakfast?"

"Cheers, see you then." Deirdre's muffled voice reached her through the door.

The clock in the hotel room said 6 a.m., but Moira's wristwatch—and evidently her body clock—was still set to Dublin time, as she was finding herself awake at quite an early hour. The morning was cool but clear and pleasant with a slight breeze. After negotiating the busy roadway in front of the hotel, she found herself on a footpath leading into a small copse of birch and pine. There were benches set here and there along the path, and she walked well into the wood before stopping at one. There was no one out and about at this hour, which was what she was hoping for—a bit of quiet to invite any Others who may be inclined to visit.

She had just settled onto a bench, taken a deep cleansing breath and closed her eyes when she felt a Presence. Evidently there was an Other who was also waiting for this right moment to appear. She opened her eyes to the welcomed sight of Nana Brigid.

"Nana! I'm so glad it's you!"

"Likewise, am I glad to see you, my dear." Her grandmother smiled. "You are certainly a long way from Erin's Isle."

"I felt as if you were sending me here. It was you who sent that dream, was it not?"

Brigid laughed, "Who else? Well, there could have been several Others, but you're right, I have been getting myself involved in this little family matter for some time now and knew you would be receptive."

"Tell me, *is* there a treasure hidden in James's barn? What is our purpose here? What can we do about this ancient family quarrel?"

"Slow down; one thing at a time," Brigid cautioned. "There are several treasures here, but perhaps not of the kind you are thinking. And yes, you will need to get into that barn, and in the state it is in, you will have to go in through the back door."

"Back door?"

"Think back to your dream. Most dreams are not so literal, but this one, ah, this one was fun to be able to add some realism. There is a root cellar under that corner of the barn that has collapsed. It has a back entrance—"

"The tree! The tree? There's a hollow tree that leads to the cellar?"

"Not exactly," Brigid laughed. "You won't need any breathing tubes; there is no water. That was only the symbol for the journey here, which you so quickly understood. Between the tree and the barn, you'll have to look for the entrance. It is quite overgrown now but look for a large stone and then slightly to the left of that you'll find the 'brass ring' so to speak. It will be up to James to decide what to do with his treasure, but I suggest you talk to him about reconciliation with the Pittsfield branch of the family, for there is more treasure out there as well."

Brigid enjoyed being cryptic and Moira knew better than to try to pry more details than her grandmother was willing or able to reveal.

"One more thing—Nuala—she's feeling a bit left out of this adventure, so I gave her a little peek into the happenings. Contact her, will you? Ask her about her dream from last night. She'll tell you it's a strange one, but I gave her a view of a dream that was sent to your cousin Katie out in Pittsfield. You haven't met her yet, but I hope you will soon."

"That's wonderful, thanks. I'll ask her right now …" As Moira turned to reach for her mobile, she barely heard a whispered, "goodbye for now, sweet girl," and looking up, found she was alone.

~

"Wear your dungarees, we could get mucky." Moira breezed into the hotel room and grabbed Deirdre, swinging her around.

"You've got news!"

"Yup, I knew Nana Brigid was behind this, but it was nice to see her and get the details—well, what little she would impart. Right now, though, I need to text Nuala; too expensive to call, but she's a part of this."

—*Hey sis, heard from Nana B that you've had a vision; not just a dream this time. You're in this thing!*

—*You're up early. Wow, cool that she told you. Her name is Katie; have you met her? Who is she?*

—*She's one of our American cousins in Pittsfield. We haven't met her yet. Hope to go out there soon. But today we dig for treasure!*

—*I'll write the vision and email it; too long to txt. Thx for the validation. B safe. <3*

∼

"These family photos are a treasure! I didn't know they had cameras that long ago." Deirdre marvelled as James spread out his collection of family memorabilia.

"That one's a tintype of a family reunion right before Thomas and Con left for the Klondike the first time, around 1895. There's my Nana Nellie holding my dad on her lap, and Con and his wife with their three kids at the time. This one is Thomas with his handlebar moustache—quite dapper. And here's my grandparents' wedding photo."

"And these letters?" Moira indicated several bundles tied with faded ribbon.

"Well, I imagine some are from your family back in the old country. Nana kept all the correspondence from back home and the few letters Thomas managed to send when he was in Alaska. Here's one he sent after he and

Con went back the second time."

Deirdre picked up the delicate pages written on letterhead of The Worcester and Northwest Mining and Trading Association and dated March 6, 1899. She read:

Dear Wife & Children hoping you are well. We are all thank God we had not a very bad winter. Have not found any thing yet we are gowing farther on soon there is not many to stay after April we are to stay the summer if I see good prospect ahead might stay next winter cant tell yet hoping will make expences very hard country to travell very slow the weather was not very bad thermometer lowest 17 below 9 ft of snow one storm 24 hours. there is but 6 of the Worcester party left after April dont be worrying about me I am all right. If I go out in the fall will have to get some money Con is gowing out I will let you know when I want money dont expect to get any letters this summer wont have much chance to send many so dont be disappointed I would like to stay with this thing to give it a good trile might strike it yet hope we will. I could write you a long letter I am telling you the facts. I hope you and the children are well and all the folks this is all I am gowing to write dont blame me for a short letter for it is the same thing day after day.

"Here's another letter written in January of the year he came back. He wrote it from Washington, after spending some time in Nome."

Deirdre read:

Fairhaven Wash Jan 15th
Dear Wife & Children

I received your letter the day I left Seattle 29th of December. I was glad to hear from you. Why dint you get Brian to write to me. I am working here; I intend to stay here for a while. I cant say how long.

There is to be a railroad build in Alaska from Valdies to Siberia. There would be a chance to make a stake in a restaurant. How would you like to run one the only thing about the children gowing to school. Nell I am gowing up to Alaska in the Spring. I will work for wages this summer. I cant save more than $1.00 a day this winter I am getting $2.25 a day and it's $5.00 a week for board. It rains a good deal here. I haven't seen no snow this winter yet and a very light frost.

I feel more homesick than before. I hate to go back without a few dollars. I will be home next fall when you write let me know how you are in money. I will send you some sometime in March. It is two bad that times are so dull in Pepperell. I suppose you could not sell the place. It took me two knights to write this letter so this letter is two knights long. Dont be lonesome but be strong and courageous. So, goodby, your husband, Thos Connolly.

"Seems kinda formal to us nowadays, signing a letter to his wife with his full name like that. Dad says he never remembers them being very affectionate to one another, but then, he was only small when his father died and he had been gone for so many years." James paused for a moment, then continued, "Nellie was fiercely loyal and stood up to Con both before and after Thomas's death, swearing there was no gold to share. If there was, we wouldn't have had so much trouble holding on to our land. Anyway, after that, the two families never spoke. It was sad, as that was all there was left to the family over here. They—*we*, should have done better … Well, what's done is done."

"That last letter sounded like he hadn't been very successful at the gold mining business but was considering relocating to run a business there," Moira said.

"That's the last letter he wrote before coming home. He went back up to Nome in March and ended up staying there until he came home that fall.

"You girls mentioned wanting to see the barn? We can't go inside due to the damage, but we can take a stroll around the yard. We had fifty acres, but now it's just this lot the house is on. I don't have anything more to sell to pay for taxes …"

"That's what we want to talk to you about—maybe as we walk out to the barn?" Moira suggested. She'd been having an internal struggle since receiving her instructions from Nana Brigid about the root cellar as to how much she should share with James. Now she felt the whole truth was the only way. What could he say? *'You're mental'* and *'get out of here'*? Well, he could say that, but they had to take that chance.

They had made their way around the north side of the barn and could see the collapsed roof and the extent of the damage. There was no way they were accessing the space from inside. As they approached that corner, Moira spied the hollow tree and the large rock next to it. There she stopped and turned to James.

"Are you aware of a root cellar entrance in this vicinity that leads under the barn?" she asked as an introduction to her bombshell.

"Root cellar? Not that I'm aware of. Why do you ask?"

Moira kicked at the leaves and dirt around the rock. Her shoe thudded and stopped against a hard object in the dirt. Stooping down, she brushed away the debris and uncovered an iron ring. "Like this right here?" she asked.

James stared at her, then bent down and pulled at the ring. It didn't budge. "How did you know this was here?" he asked incredulously. As he began clearing away the layers of dead leaves, dirt and moss that covered the wooden entrance, Moira began her explanation.

"James, I don't want you to be alarmed, but I have a special connection with people—especially those in my family—who have passed over to the Otherworld. I use this gift to help people in ways that can't be accomplished any other way. Deirdre and I came here because my grandmother Brigid told me you needed help. I think this root cellar is the repository of something your grandfather Thomas brought back from Alaska and then it got forgotten, or he couldn't or didn't communicate that to his wife and brother before he died—what? What is it? Why are you laughing?" Moira stopped, confused by James's reaction.

"I know that woman! Your grandmother, Brigid, you say? It must be her who's been visiting me in dreams these past few days, bugging the heck out of me. I kept telling myself that it was my poor digestion giving me grief at night, but she showed me this very spot, over and over every night for the past three nights. She'd tell me to follow her. She said her name was Brigid and she was going to help me. I told her I didn't need help but she ignored me and walked outside. I'd follow her and each time she'd come to this spot, point at the ground, and then poof! She'd be gone. Ha! I'm not crazy after all!"

James slapped his knees with both hands and said, "Well what are we waiting for?" He hustled back into the house, leaving Moira and Deirdre to look at each other in astonishment. "Well, that was easy," Deirdre said. Looking up into the sky, she said, "Thanks, Nana B."

James was back in a few minutes with a crowbar, saw, and hammer. "Wasn't sure which would best do the job, so I brought what I could find."

"Let's try the crowbar on the ring, and if that doesn't work, we can use it on the wood around it." Deirdre grabbed the crowbar and fitted the curved end under the ring. With both she and Moira pulling, it creaked and groaned a bit, but didn't come free.

"If it leads to a root cellar that's accessible through the barn, it may be locked from the inside." James stepped cautiously on the exposed wood and it sagged slightly under his weight. "This is very unstable; the wood is old and rotted around the edges. It should be easily broken up, but be careful not to fall through it in the process."

He took the crowbar from Deirdre and pried it under a board near the edge. With a terrible shriek of splintering wood, he fell backwards in a heap, but he had succeeded in prying loose one of the boards.

"Are you alright?" Both girls ran to his side and grasping his hands, pulled James up from the ground.

"Ayah, I'm fine. Thanks."

With a bit more caution this time, they worked the wood and as another board came out, they heard a clink of metal against stone. Looking into the newly opened hole, they saw a small slide lock lying on a stone step leading into darkness. With the lock dislodged, the iron ring pulled up what remained of the cellar door.

"Ladies first," James said, bowing gallantly. He had also brought a flashlight and handed it to Moira, who gingerly stepped onto the stone sill.

"The ceiling is low, you have to stoop a bit, but it's not bad," she called over her shoulder as Deirdre and James followed her in.

"Ugh! Cobwebs. Yuck!"

"Thanks for breaking them up for us, Mo," Deirdre called out from behind her.

Moira grumbled, "Don't mention it."

It wasn't very far to the door at the other end, and this one was not locked. As she pulled it open, Moira saw the space behind illuminated somewhat by the outlines of the trap door to the barn above. With the roof caved in, daylight filtered down and revealed a small, five metres square room, dug out of the earth. Two rows of wooden shelves went up chest-high on three of the packed-earth walls. They were all bare except for a metal strongbox on the top centre shelf.

Chapter Twenty-One

"All argument is against it; but all belief is for it."

—Samuel Johnson on the existence of ghosts, from *Boswell's Life of Samuel Johnson*

"It doesn't feel very heavy," Deirdre observed as the three of them sat at James's kitchen table with the box in front of them.

"Only one way to find out," James declared as he pulled the box closer to him. It was a simple clasp latch, but as he tried to flip it up over the hasp, it wouldn't budge. "Okay, we need a knife to pry it open," he said as he went to the silverware drawer.

"Wait, do you have any lubricant? Maybe try that first," Moira suggested.

"Good idea." James opened the cabinet under the sink and pulled out the can. Squirting some liberally on and around the clasp, he waited a moment, then easily lifted the lid. Inside there were three objects: a key with a string attached to it with a faded tag, and two small chamois drawstring bags. James took all three out and laid them on the table. He opened the drawstring of one of the bags and poured out into his palm about a quarter cup of gold dust with several gold nuggets nestled in it. The second bag contained the same.

"Look!" Deirdre had turned the bags over, and in faded ink on the chamois cloth was handwritten, 'Brian' on one, and 'Greg' on the other. "Presents for his children," she said softly.

Moira picked up the key. She fingered the tag attached to it and saw the faint number 333 printed on it. "This could be a safety deposit key." She held the key up to the light and squinted, "It's got the initials 'WFUT' on it. Wonder what that means?"

"Wells Fargo Bank. It used to be called the Wells Fargo & Union Trust," James explained. "It's the bank our family has always used. Do you think Thomas put his gold in the bank here in town?"

There was a split second of silence before three chairs pushed away from the table and they were out the door. "Your car or mine?" Moira called out.

"Hop in the truck," James said, heading for the beat-up Ford pickup truck in the drive. "You know what they say about bankers' hours? If we hurry, we can make it in time before they close for lunch."

~

"It's not our key. We don't have that many safe deposit boxes. The key number would have to be below 250." Matthew Woodward, the bank representative, offered the key back to James. "But you're right, it is a Wells Fargo key."

"What are the chances it could be a bank in Alaska?" Deirdre speculated.

"That's a good guess," Moira agreed. "Is there any way you could check with other branches, maybe in Nome, or…" Turning to James she asked, "What other places did Thomas mention?"

"Yakutat? Seattle?" James suggested.

"Definitely in Seattle and Nome; they are big enough cities. I highly doubt there's a branch in Yakutat, but I will look into this. I'm not sure of the protocol here. I'll have to check with my manager and get back to you."

With nothing else to be done, they wrote down their contact information, the details of the key, and Thomas' and Cornelius' names and the approximate periods they were in Alaska.

"Now what?" asked Deirdre as the three left the bank.

"Hey, I can take you by the cemetery and you can visit all the family we got buried there," James suggested.

"Grand!" they both said at once.

Chapter Twenty-Two

'No man ever wore a cravat as nice as his own child's arm around his neck.'
—Irish Proverb

"Is this Mr James Connolly?" The voice on the line inquired.

"You got 'im," James replied.

"This is Matthew Woodward. We met at the bank this morning?"

"Ah, yes, right." James motioned for Deirdre and Moira to listen in as he put the phone on speaker. "You've got news already?"

"I do. The Seattle branch came up empty, but in Nome, we struck gold—ha-ha! Figuratively, that is, let's not get ahead of ourselves…ahem. Anyway, their records show a safe deposit box taken out in October of 1902 by Thomas Connolly."

"That's amazing! We just need to get up there to retrieve it?" James asked.

"It's not that easy. After this long a time, the contents of the safe deposit box are turned over to the Alaska Department of Revenue Treasury Division in Juneau. They have a website for submitting claims …"

As Matthew Woodward provided contact information and instructions, Moira wrote it down for James. When he hung up, they all began talking at once:

"Well, I'll be! What do you think?"

"We need to go there …"

"You should contact the Cornelius branch about this …"

"Hold on, hold on." Moira held up her hand for silence. "Let's call this number first and see what the next step will be."

After several long bouts of being on hold and a few transfers to different departments, they learned that since James was a descendant of the alleged owner, and not the actual owner, he needed to supply a death certificate for Thomas, birth certificates for himself and his father, a death certificate for his father, and copies of any wills designating himself or his father, heir to Thomas' estate. Having the safety box key was only the beginning, but certainly helpful.

"That's a tall order," Deirdre assessed. "Where do we start looking for those items?"

"Thomas didn't leave a will that I know of, but with my father as his only living child, everything went first to Nellie then to Dad. I have a copy of my dad's will. He gave me the house here and its contents, and five thousand dollars to each of my sisters."

"What about the birth and death certificates? Do you have copies of those?" Moira asked.

"No." As he noted their stricken expressions he added, "But I know where to get them. Our family lived and died right here in Pepperell; the town clerk should have all that on file."

"James, the Alaskan Revenue website says you can upload all these documents online, but you must appear in person to claim the contents. How do you feel about a trip to Juneau?" Moira already knew how *she* felt, and was ready to hit the road for Alaska, but this was James' inheritance.

"Ack! I'm seventy-five years old. My old bones won't survive a trip like that; and neither will my pocketbook." James seemed so discouraged after the elation of earlier.

"You don't look a day over seventy!" Deirdre said. "But I think it's time we brought in family reinforcements," Deirdre surmised. "Do you have contact information for your relatives in Pittsfield? And you should call your daughters as well."

"I have my grandson Alex's phone number. I can call him and ask for his parents' number."

Just then, James' phone rang. Caller ID said 'Alex.'

"It's my grandson," James said.

"Heya Gramps, Alex here."

"Alex, how are you?"

"Doing pretty well. Hey, I would like to come visit you tomorrow. Will you be home in the afternoon?"

"Sure thing; I've some friends here I'd like you to meet when you come." James raised his eyebrows as he looked at Deirdre and Moira who nodded that they would be available to meet Alex.

"I have someone I would like you to meet as well."

After their conversation ended, Moira said, "Shall we let you take care of getting those documents together? We'll be back here tomorrow."

"That's some coincidence that Alex would want to come by right when we were talking about reaching out to family, eh?" James said.

"There's no such thing as coincidence," Deirdre and Moira said in unison, and all three laughed.

Chapter Twenty-Three

"Women are the voices of that Otherworld, which is so perfectly entangled with this one. They have been the prophets, oracles and conduits through which the Otherworld could speak."

—Dr. Sharon Blackie

"Gramps, good to see you," Alex said as he embraced the old man tenderly. There were tears in James' eyes as he was folded into his grandson's arms. "I'd like you to meet Katie, my fiancée."

James stepped back from Alex and took in the petite brunette with the dancing green eyes. Katie smiled and stepping forward, held out her hand to him, but he stood still and continued to stare.

"Gramps?" Alex questioned.

"Have we met before? You look very familiar …"

"I don't think so. I've heard a lot about you from

Alex, but no, we haven't met," Katie said.

"I've got it!" James turned around abruptly and hustled back into the house, leaving his guests on the front porch, where they all looked tentatively from one to another.

Deirdre took the initiative and put her hand out to Alex. "I'm Deirdre Gallagher, and this is my sister, Moira. We are visiting from Ireland."

"Ireland! How do you know my grandfather?"

"Well, actually, we're related," Moira joined the conversation.

A slow smile spread across Alex's face. He ran his fingers through his hair and said, "You don't say; It would appear that relatives are coming out of the woodwork these days."

"What do you mean?" Moira asked. But the question went unanswered as James returned grasping his box of family photos in both hands.

"Here. That photo I showed you girls of the last family reunion held here at the farm. There she is, right there—Cornelius' wife, Méabl McCarthy Connolly. Katie's the spitting image."

"Good eye, Gramps! There is somewhat of a family resemblance there. Katie is Méabl's great-granddaughter."

"Alex and I are third cousins, "Katie added. "That's kissing cousins, of course …"

"Oh my! Well, come in, come in. Sounds like we all have a lot to talk about." James began introducing Moira and Deirdre but they all assured him that introductions had been made and followed him into the front room.

Alex began the tale. "Katie and I met at school. Well, it was a college mixer Trivia Night. We were randomly placed on the same team. Between the two of us, we wiped out the competition and walked away with the first prize of a meal at a local restaurant. I wasted no time in setting up that date and by the time dessert came around, I was smitten."

Katie took up the narrative. "We dated for over a year before we got around to talking about our families and our ancestry. The more we compared notes, the more we saw we had a lot in common. I mean *a lot* in common. When we got to the family story of our great-grandfathers going to the Klondike to search for gold, there was no doubt we were related.

"I was so upset that I didn't see Alex for a couple weeks even though he called every day. I did a lot of research and that's when I discovered that the relationship of third cousins is an acceptable relationship for a marriage. And we had been talking marriage at that point."

"Meanwhile, I talked to my mom about it," Alex said. "I asked her why I didn't know anything about the other Connolly relatives in the area. She brushed it aside saying it was ancient history and why did I want to know about that? I *should* have told her right then about Katie, but I didn't—"

"Well, it was the same with me," Katie interrupted. "I knew there had been some kind of falling out, but we never talked about it. My family had already met and loved Alex, so I shouldn't have been so timid."

"The time was right to tell our plans to the family. Last weekend Katie's parents hosted a family reunion at their place on the lake. Katie and I had each gotten a job offer in Alaska and planned to get married this summer and then be in Alaska by September."

"All this worrying for nothing. My parents were so happy for us, and when we told them about our common ancestry, Mom said it was about time we healed that rift and said she would call you, James. I asked her to wait until we had visited you, but you can expect to hear from her soon. I hope that's okay?"

James let out a loud guffaw, "Okay? It's more than okay." Then it was James's turn to tell his story of the lost and found treasure of the Connolly brothers.

When James had finished, Alex asked, "Tell me Gramps, what is your plan for retrieving the contents of that safe-deposit box?"

"I don't know ... I don't know. That's a long plane ride, and an even longer car trip. I don't have the means to afford a trip like that, either." James shook his head at the thought.

"Well, maybe I—*we* could do it for you. Katie and I will be in Nome starting in the fall. She'll be head of the music department for the school district there, and I'll be the speech therapist, though my territory will be quite a bit wider than Nome and will involve a bit of travel. You could designate me your Power of Attorney and we would take care of it for you."

"That's something we could do? That's amazing about your jobs, congratulations; what a coinci—" James stopped himself and looked at Deirdre and Moira, who smiled. "Never mind; there's no such thing as a coincidence!" he finished.

Suddenly, Katie got a look of intense concentration as she stared at Moira. "Moira ... Moira ... I've heard about you."

"And I have heard about you as well," Moira smiled. "You are a Dreamer, are you not?"

Both young women began to laugh, and it was quite some time before they were settled enough to tell the tale of Katie's Moon Trip and her cousin, Nuala's peek into that vision from across the ocean.

"I was so conflicted about our plans before that dream. I knew my parents wanted me to take a local job to be near them. They've never been that encouraging about a career in music and that, combined with telling them about our relationship and shared ancestry ... it was causing so much anxiety and self-doubt."

"Let me get this straight," Alex mused. "You think our ancestors may have had something to do with all this?" He waved his arms as if to encompass them, the room, and the world around them.

"I know my Nana Brigid was a formidable presence in this life and, as far as I can tell, wields no small amount of influence in the Otherworld as well. I can only surmise from the summit meeting on the Moon that *your* Wise Mothers are just as powerful and influential," Moira said.

"They are bound to us and we to them. Their love, concern and intervention on our behalf transcends death and time," Deirdre added.

"I love that," Katie exclaimed. "I thought at first that my Moon Dream was only that, a dream, but the interactions were so real, and I felt this pure love emanating from all three of those angelic women. I know in my heart that you are absolutely correct, and it gives me such peace to know they are there watching over us."

~

"I wish we could stay to attend the wedding, but we have to get back home," Moira began. "We'd like to be with you when James finally meets with your families."

"The plan is to have another family get-together at our place next weekend, for James and my parents to get together, and for Alex's parents to meet my folks." Katie grasped each of their hands in hers. "It's been amazing to meet you and to have your support and help on this journey. Are you sure you can't put off your return to Ireland for one more week?"

"I wish!" Moira enthused, "but we do need to get back home. Please keep in touch and let us know how things turn out in Nome, and what the contents are of that safe deposit box."

"And know that you are always welcome to come to Ireland anytime and see your family there as well," Deirdre added.

Chapter Twenty-Four

*"Here's to your roof, may it be well thatched
And here's to all under it—May they be well matched."*

—Irish Toast

Subject: Connolly Clan Update

Katie Connolly Stone

To: me

August 23, 2010 3:30 pm

Greetings Cousins,

Sorry not to have written for so long, but it has been a whirlwind summer. The wedding was perfect, Mom and Alex's mother, Ella, and her sister, Amelia were a dynamic trio in organizing everything. You'd think they had been a team of wedding planners their whole lives.

Anyway, here we are up in Nome. Alex and I stopped in Juneau on the way here as planned and went to the Alaska Department of Treasury and, are you ready for this?? The safe deposit box contained quite a few gold nuggets! James authorized us to convert it to dollars and he and my dad split it down the middle. There was enough for James to pay his back taxes on the farm with some left over.

But the biggest surprise was a deed to property in Nome! Always the Irish Way to value the land, and I guess Thomas thought their 'treasure' was best invested in land. There's about 40 acres of good real estate outside of the city limits of Nome, which means, it has not been subject to property taxes. After a discussion between the family heads, they decided to give it to us for a wedding gift. They said it was our union that brought the greatest gift of reuniting our families and wanted to "invest" the land in our future. Part of Dad's inheritance is going towards building a little cabin here for us to begin our family.

They also agreed that if it hadn't been for you, they would never have known about any of this and are sending you a reward as a finder's fee of sorts, since you wouldn't accept any payment for services rendered, ha-ha.

You have opened our eyes to the importance and blessing of family and given us back not only our own extended family here, but also showed us the greater family ties we have back in the Old Country as well as the family we are still connected to on the Otherworld. We will be forever grateful.

Alex just told me that James is planning to sell the property in Pepperell now that it is free and clear, and pay for renovations at Amelia's home in Springfield to include a "father-in-law" suite for him to move down there. Amelia and Ella live close, so he will be looked after and loved by his children and grandchildren. Such a sweet man.

We hope to see you again, if not here in Nome, then perhaps a honeymoon trip for us in Ireland!

With much love,

Katie (& Alex)

BOOK THREE
WE ARE HAUNTED

(Tá faitíos orainn)

Chapter Twenty-Five

Ní lugha an fhroig ná mátíiair an uilc.
'Evil may spring from the tiniest thing.'
—Irish Proverb

August 24, 2010, Former McGuire Stud Farm, County Kildare, Ireland

"Notice the large, welcoming foyer; so much light!" Meredith Hodnett had pasted on her best estate agent smile—the one she pulled out when she was trying her best to spin a hopeless situation into a potential dream home. This was only the second showing for the place, but she got the same uneasy vibe this time as she had last week when she came with that nice American couple. There was something not right here. Fine, she'll admit it—it gave her the creeps. It all *looked* elegant, fancy, stately even, but it didn't *feel* right.

Oh, she knew about the folks who used to own it—the McGuires—both dead from a car accident. Not that she believed in ghosts; of course not. It was fun to pretend on Samhain that ghosts and goblins were about, but that was all make-believe.

"What was that? Sorry, I was thinking of something ... you were saying?" Meredith turned her attention to the portly gentleman and his timid wife who were in the market for "something big ... you know, grand and showy."

"The plumbing—basement, heating unit, pipes—I'd like to see what condition they're in."

"Of course; this way." Meredith led them towards an unobtrusive door underneath the staircase. As if on cue, there came a groaning and rumbling from below as they approached: pipes clanking, a piercing whistle, and a low rumble like the approach of a distant freight train. The woman's eyes widened as she looked to her husband.

"What the heck ...?" He pushed past Meredith and yanked on the doorknob. It appeared to be stuck, so he pulled all the harder, to no avail. With one more heroic effort, he pulled with both hands and the door slid open easily, catching the man off balance and sending him flying backwards, landing with a thud on the floor.

"Oh, Mr. Murray! I'm so sorry. Are you hurt?" Meredith hurried over to the now red-faced Murray, offering him a helping hand, which he waved off as he clambered to his feet.

"I'm fine, fine," he blustered. "What kind of a blasted trick was that?" Approaching the basement door once again, he opened and shut it several times with ease. No sound emanated from the other side, so they all trooped down the stairs for a look. Nothing seemed out of order, the systems running as they were intended, with no indication of from where or what the noises had come.

Meredith assured the Murrays that she would get an inspector to go through the systems, and the rest of the tour proceeded uneventfully. But the Murrays' initial enthusiasm for the place was gone and Meredith knew they were just going through the motions with a "let's get this over with" attitude. There would be no sale. The mood of the place had gotten to them as well.

They said their goodbyes in the drive, and as Meredith turned to her own vehicle, she sensed movement from an upstairs window. Looking up, she saw a pale hand holding back the drapery and caught a brief glimpse of a figure looking down at her. Before she could see more, the curtain fell back into place.

∼

"Haunted! Are you joking?" Seán paced in a tight circle around his kitchen as he tried to grasp what his estate agent was suggesting.

"I'm sorry, Mr Kennedy, I don't know what else to think. Perhaps someone has broken into the house? Does anyone else have a key? Or, someone is playing a practical joke on you." Meredith knew it was balmy to even propose that ghosts were to blame for the strange things that seemed to happen every time she went out to the McGuire-now-Kennedy estate. But she had gotten several negative reports from other agents as well, and now most of them were reluctant to show it at all.

"Okay, I'll head over there myself this afternoon and check it out. Thanks for letting me know."

Seán couldn't believe what he had just heard. It had been a little over a month since he'd gotten the keys and all the documentation to establish ownership. The probate process had taken almost a year, and in all that time he hadn't been able to set foot on the property.

At first, he had intended to move in, do some renovating, start up the stud farm again. After all, he still owned the horses that came with the estate. They had been temporarily (now, for over a year) stabled at a neighbouring farm, but he had high hopes of making a go of it. He'd spent the last year researching the industry and learning all he could about the business. During his teen years he'd worked for a farmer who had a few horses, so he at least felt comfortable around the animals. As soon as he began formulating the plan to run the stud farm, he'd hired on at a nearby stud operation to get a more thorough look at the process. He knew there was a lot he didn't know, and hoped to surround himself with a knowledgeable support team.

When he'd finally been able to go and check out the estate, he *had* felt overcome by feelings of apprehension and foreboding, but he put it down to the condition of things: overgrown with weeds and overshadowed by neglect. That, coupled with the flood of emotions as he thought of his mother living here and feeling helpless and hopeless at the mercy of a merciless husband, began to weigh on him. It wasn't long before he'd had second thoughts. He'd decided to see if he could sell it off quickly instead.

Selling "as is" meant he couldn't list it at the high end of the market, but he couldn't face the prospects of renovations and repairs. Was he now going to be stuck with a haunted house no one would buy? It was rubbish. Utter nonsense. He would get to the bottom of what was going on.

∼

The entrance was certainly impressive. Seán had to stop and swing open the iron gate before continuing on the unpaved drive. Despite the weeds pushing up along the centre, the drive was graded and relatively smooth. Seán clocked it at a good half-kilometre, lined with birch, alder, and rowan trees already starting to turn colour. They formed a canopy overhead as their branches intertwined above. He could see ash and oak as well further back in the wood. At the edge of the wood, a hedgerow of elder grew on either side of the opening. The drive continued on past a small stone cottage on the left. Seán assumed it was for a groundskeeper or caretaker of some sort, and his original plan of settling in there while doing renovations pricked at the back of his mind. He brushed it aside as the main house came into view.

The drive became cobblestones as it curved in a semi-circle approaching the entrance. A circular garden bed of weeds sat forlornly opposite. Again, he was struck with a feeling of melancholy as he drove up to the front door. It looked more like a hunting lodge than a home—a towering structure of grey stone that matched the cottage, and ivy climbed and clung to one side. Two rounded turrets complete with arrow-slit windows stood sentinel at each end of the building. It was a vanity, of course. He didn't know the exact date of construction, but he was pretty sure it wasn't medieval; closer to the mid-1800s. Old enough, though, to house a ghost or two ... He could see where the appearance of the place lent itself to wild imaginings.

His key fit into the brass lock set into the huge oak door. There was a second key inside the lockbox for the use of estate agents showing the house, but he had his own and the door swung open on well-oiled hinges—one of the few things he had gotten to before deciding to list the house. The other was to hire a cleaning crew to attack the years' worth of cobwebs and dust. Now that he thought back on that, it had taken several calls to quite a few cleaning agencies before he found one willing to take on the job. None had mentioned hauntings as a reason to decline, but would they have said? He made a mental note to visit a local pub and drop some leading comments to see what he could learn.

Where to start—top to bottom or bottom to top? He didn't know much about plumbing and heating systems but they couldn't be that complicated. The agent had reported on the noises from the basement so he headed in that direction. The door opened easily, unlike poor Mr. Murray's experience. He could tell that the cleaning crew hadn't ventured down here, but it wasn't too bad, for a cellar. The wine bottles lining the shelves of the alcove were dusty, and he could see evidence of mice. There was probably a small fortune in wine alone that would go far in helping with renovations. In the furnace room he found the latest inspection report dated two days ago along with the service report that he had ordered from last month. Nothing unusual here.

He started back towards the stairs when the lights flickered for a moment then went out completely. He hadn't thought to bring a flashlight down with him, though he had one in the boot. Lot of good it was doing him there. He froze in place getting his bearings, hoping his eyes would soon adjust to the dark. Maybe it wasn't furnace issues, but something electrical? Then, in the stillness he heard a whisper—not words, exactly, more like air escaping lips. A sense of dread came over him as all the stories the agent had related came into his mind: strange sounds, a shadowy presence, doorlatches with minds of their own. He must be imagining things. That's what being in the dark and disoriented will do—there! Again ... whispered words this time, *"help me."*

Chapter Twenty-Six

*'He who has water and peat on his own farm
has the world his own way.'*
—Irish proverb

The lights came on and Seán wasted no time scrambling up the steps to the foyer. He decided that was enough of an inspection for the time being. He exited the front door, and with shaking hands, locked it. Was he trying to keep whatever *that* was inside? He got in his vehicle but didn't drive off immediately. Taking time to think, he began rationalizing what had occurred. What *had* occurred? A faulty wiring connection? An active imagination? What was to be his next move?

As if in answer to his own question, an image of a young woman came into his mind; a lovely young woman, as he recalled. Had it been eight months since he'd last spoken to Nuala? Why hadn't he pursued a relationship, when he'd gotten a feeling that she might be interested in him as well? He'd called her a few times after Christmas, and they'd chatted a bit, but she had gone off to culinary school, and he was busy trying to educate himself for his future. He hoped it wasn't too late. And now, this was a perfect opener to be in touch. He would ask her if she and her sisters might help him look into the possibility that his new home was haunted.

The idea of entering the house with reinforcements sounded like a much better plan than trying to figure out what was happening on his own. He could feel his breathing slow and his heartbeat returning to its normal rhythm after the adrenaline rush of trying to get out of the house faster than his legs could carry him.

~

Nuala looked down at her mobile as it trilled an incoming call. Seán Kennedy. Hmm. It'd been a while; what could he want?

"Hello?"

"Nuala! Great to hear your voice! How ya getting on? This is Seán …"

"I'm grand, yourself?"

"That's the thing … ah, sorry it's been so long since

I called. I meant to … I should've …"

"It's fine, I could've called you as well—this isn't Victorian England, after all. I'm really glad you called."

"You are? That's grand. And your sisters? Are they alright? Are they still in the investigating business?"

"I'm actually a partner in the business now as well. We all have our different skills to contribute—"

"Ah, sound. Cheers for that. And school? Are you finished with the cooking classes?"

"Oh, that was only for four months. I graduated last spring," she said, hinting at the amount of time that had passed since they had last spoken. "I've been chef here at the inn ever since."

"And Moira and Deirdre? They're pretty busy with their investigations business?"

What was he going on about? "Seán, did you call for a specific reason? As much as I enjoy talking with you, it doesn't sound like you just called to chat." Nuala would rather he got to the point, if there was a point.

"Right. You're right. Here goes. I need your and your sisters' help. Again."

The tale came pouring out. Seán was relieved to be able to talk about what was happening with someone whom he knew wouldn't ridicule, would understand, wouldn't think he was a nutter. As he spoke, Nuala remembered how comfortable she was talking to Seán. And she had to admit, she was thoroughly hooked at the idea of investigating a haunted house. Deirdre and Moira would be thrilled.

"Do ya think you can fit me into the schedule?" Seán asked as he finished his story.

"I was just checking the calendar and it looks like nothing is going on Friday afternoon—that's two days from now, is that soon enough?"

"Bang on! We could meet at the estate, say around two o'clock?"

"I'll need to check with Deirdre and Moira, of course, but assume it's fine unless you hear back from me."

"Thanks, Nuala. I appreciate it. See you Friday."

"Fine then. Love you, bye."

"Umm …"

But whatever he was going to say, Nuala didn't hear, as she disconnected the line immediately upon realizing what she had said. She was mortified. Had she really, unthinkingly, ended the call with their family sign-off of 'love you, bye'? Could she ever even look at him again? What would she say?

Chapter Twenty-Seven

Fada iarsma na droichbheirte.
'The effects of an evil act are long felt.'
—Irish Proverb

That Friday afternoon, the four converged on the estate in Kildare. Seán held the passenger door as Nuala unfolded herself from the back seat of her sister's Mini, and took her hand to assist.

Nuala looked up at him and smiled. No awkwardness here. The conversation they'd had soon after the "love you" slip had cleared the air and they were able to laugh about it.

"So, you ladies ready for the grand tour?"

"Lead the way," Moira said with enthusiasm.

"Wow, this is pure class!" Nuala exclaimed as they entered the cathedral-ceilinged foyer. Perhaps her bias towards Seán was colouring her enthusiasm, but she did feel drawn to the place.

"Shhhh. Be still for a moment. I'd like to get my bearings and a sense of things before we move ahead." Moira had her hand on the banister, her eyes were closed, and she breathed in deeply a few times. "There's definitely a vibration here that is indicative of a presence." A moment passed and she said, "I'm good. Where to, Seán?"

"I think I want to start upstairs this time." He led the way up the staircase. At the top, a corridor led off in two directions.

"Shall we divide and conquer? Seán and Nuala take the left and Moira and I'll go right. There are so many rooms; it will take us forever if we stick together," Deirdre reasoned.

They all agreed, but before they filed off to explore, Seán turned to Moira and asked, "But what are we looking for? I mean, I can tell if someone has been camping out or if there is a broken window where someone got in, but I brought you in for your expertise in more paranormal matters. How can we tell if there is … what did you say earlier? A presence?"

"Hmm. Good question. It's more about feelings. Haven't you ever felt as if someone behind you was staring at you? Or you think about a certain person and they call you right then? Be open to impressions. Tap into your sixth sense. Also, note unusual smells, sounds—"

"Oh, I know about that one. You noticed we didn't start in the basement?"

"Right, we know someone is here; someone who is reaching out and wants help. We just need to be open to how they want to approach us."

As they separated, Moira suggested they take photos in each room for later reference.

Once on their own, Moira said to Deirdre, "Was this your attempt at matchmaking?"

"Was it that obvious? All Nuala could talk about last night and on the way over here was 'Seán this' and 'Seán that.'"

"That's my point. I don't think they need any help from us."

"Point taken."

As they moved from room to room, they saw large pieces of heavy, old-fashioned furniture, paintings and bric-a-brac, but nothing that looked suspicious.

They regrouped at the head of the stairs after about twenty minutes.

"Anything unusual?" Seán asked.

"Looked like mostly bedrooms our way. A couple office-type areas and two bathrooms," Deidre said. "Nothing seemed disturbed or out of place," she added.

"The rooms on our side were mostly servants' quarters

or storage rooms," Seán said. "There's a lot of old junk I can't wait to get rid of. I'd meant to have an estate sale before now, but then I decided to sell it as is."

"But did anybody *feel* anything?" Moira asked.

"Cold," said Nuala. "It's icy cold up here."

"Nuala's right, and it shouldn't be. The heating system has been recently checked and cleaned." Seán frowned.

"Well, a cold chill often does accompany a visitation. Maybe our friend is close by after all," Moira said.

"Any preferences as to whether we tackle the basement or the towers next?" Seán asked.

"Oooh, the towers! They look so romantic!" Nuala exclaimed and then blushed.

"Towers it is. Since they are so far apart, I suggest we stick together, if that's fine with you all," Seán said, and led the way to a small door at the end of one of the corridors.

It was dark in the stairwell, with the only light coming from the slit windows placed periodically in the curve of the outer wall.

"I can't imagine what this was used for. Do you know, Seán?" Deirdre asked.

"I don't. There's an empty room at the top. Mostly designed for looks from the outside, is my guess."

They trudged up in silence for a while, until Nuala, in front and reaching the top first, exclaimed exultantly,

"Fifty-five!"

"Yeah?" Deirdre said, "that's interesting."

"What? Why? What's the meaning of fifty-five?" Nuala asked.

"Well, it's the number for change, transformation and freedom. It signifies the beginning of new relationships and connections."

"You're making that up," Nuala charged, blushing again.

"I don't joke about numerology."

Nuala turned her back on them and tried the door to the tower room. It didn't budge.

"Here, let me try." Seán pulled out his ring of keys and inserted one into the lock. It clicked and he pushed it open. They all went in and stood glancing around the empty, circular room. The walls were stone on the inside as well with a heavy casing of wood around the one window.

"Not much to see in here," Seán observed.

"Down here—look." Moira was pointing to a spot under the window. There appeared to be scratch marks on the stone. Now she was down on the floor peering closer at the scratches. "They are hash marks, in different sets. This grouping has five. Under that is a series of seven. Here there are six more."

"If this were a prison, that would indicate how

many days a person was confined here," Deirdre said and shuddered. "Do you think someone *was* shut up in here?"

"This place is creepy," Nuala said. "Let's go back down."

"You all go ahead. I'm going to stay a moment longer. Sometimes spirits are reluctant to appear before a crowd. Maybe if it's just me here, they will feel more comfortable," Moira said.

"Well, don't be long," Deirdre cautioned.

The three made their way down the steep stairs and were almost at the bottom when they heard a loud bang. The sound reverberated through the stone tower.

"What was that?" Nuala looked back up into the tower.

"MOIRA!" Deirdre called out. She turned around and sprinted up the steps. She arrived breathless to find the door to the room shut and unyielding. "Moira, are you alright?"

"I'm fine. The door slammed shut and now it won't open. Is Seán there with the key?"

"He's coming, I'm sure. I beat them to the top." Turning around she shouted down the stairs, "Seán, we need the key!"

"Coming."

Seán arrived with the key already in hand, but after several fruitless attempts to get the key to turn in the lock, he offered, "Maybe we need some oil. I have a can in my car. Will you be alright for a few minutes, Moira?"

"Sure, I'm fine."

"I'll be right back."

While he was gone, Moira spoke to her sisters on the other side of the door.

"After you left, there were two presences that appeared almost at the same time, as if they were vying for attention, or antagonistic to each other. I couldn't see them, but they were giving off different vibes. The one, less menacing and more urgent, seemed to be coming through first when the door blasted shut; I'm assuming at the instigation of the other, darker presence."

"Are they gone now?" Nuala asked.

"I'm definitely alone here."

It seemed to the sisters that it took forever, but Seán arrived with the lubricant in less than ten minutes. "Don't be looking through the keyhole now, Moira, while I spray this."

"I've stepped back. Go ahead."

Seán sprayed into the lock and around the doorframe where the bolt would slide. He turned the handle and gave it a good push. Nothing.

"Oh no, oh no! Now what do we do?" Nuala was close to tears.

"Think, think—Moira, did you hear or notice anything unusual when the door slammed? Is the window open at all?" Deirdre had begun pacing in a tight circle, as much as would allow with the three of them on the small landing.

"The window's closed. The latch is rusted shut. It hasn't been opened in a long time, is my guess."

"So, no breeze blew it shut …"

"Wait, I did hear something. There was a slight clicking sound right after the door slammed. I ran to it and that's when I heard it—a soft click, like a latch going into place."

"What's this?" Deirdre was running her hand over an area to the left of the door. There was a circular spot about a half-inch in diameter and slightly off-colour from the stone around it. She pressed her finger on it. They all heard the click near the door handle.

Nuala immediately tried the handle and the door swung open. She ran into the room and fiercely hugged her sister. Moira laughed and patted her back. "I'm grand, really."

"What do you see?" Deirdre directed her question to Seán, who was on his knees peering into the doorframe.

"It's a neat trick. This metal rod slides in and out of the door as you press on the access point outside the door.

Like a bolt lock, but this looks like it was installed with the original building. There's no way to work it from the inside. It can only be operated on the outside, ensuring that even if a person in the room had a key, they couldn't get out without help from someone on the other side of the door." He stood up and looked at the girls. "I think this *was* built to be a prison."

"It's well camouflaged. You'd have to know it was there and be looking for it. Evidently, our ghost knew it was there," Deirdre said.

They exited the room and went down in subdued silence. Once in the main part of the house, Seán said, "I think I'll look into the deed history and see if I can trace to the original owners. I'd like to know who built this place and learn a bit more about its past."

"You mean, what kind of person builds a tower prison in their home?" Deirdre asked.

"Exactly."

"You might want to start with Griffith's Valuation. I believe that covers the years 1847-1864," Nuala said.

Moira and Deidre stared at their little sister.

"What? Ma uses that all the time to help with her genealogical research. I've been helping her—well, she's been teaching me—and I've learned a lot. It's fascinating."

"That's ... good to know," Deirdre said.

"I say we go outside a bit and get some fresh air." Moira was already headed for the front entrance as she spoke.

"Sound idea. I can give you a tour of the gardens and stables if you'd like." Seán led them around the side of the house to the iron gate which led to the stables, pasture, and gardens. There was no lock here and he swung it open on creaking hinges. A gravel path led past a kitchen garden at the back of the house and on towards the stables.

Deirdre stopped at the kitchen garden. "There are still things growing here. Let's see …" She began to meander through the rows of overgrown perennial herbs that were already gone to seed. "Look, Moira, here's holy basil, and feverfew, calendula … and that rosemary bush is huge!" She and Moira lingered while Seán and Nuala continued on towards the stables.

As they walked, Seán said, "It's so good to see you … and your sisters, of course …" This time it was Seán who blushed.

Nuala laughed lightly. "I like you, Seán, and it's good to see you, too."

Emboldened, Seán said, "I'm not so good with people. I envy your relationships with your sisters; and with your ma, too. You all seem to really like each other and can talk about things easily. I've been alone for most of my life."

"But the Kennedys—how long have they been gone?"

"Oh, only a couple years, but they weren't the touchy-feely type. I've always known I was adopted. They were good to me, took care of me, but I always knew I wasn't their 'real' son."

"That's so sad."

"Being an only child, I missed out on sibling relationships. I don't know … I'm much more comfortable around computers than people."

"Are you comfortable around me?"

"Aye, that's what I'm trying to say. I feel like I can talk to you and you understand me."

Moira and Deidre caught up with them as they approached the stables.

"That kitchen garden is amazing! I took some cuttings; I hope you don't mind, Seán," Deirdre said.

"Help yourself. Glad something good can come of this place."

"Now, Seán, we'll figure this out, don't worry. It will all work out," Moira said.

Deirdre and Nuala glanced at each other and smiled at Moira's eternal optimism.

Chapter Twenty-Eight

*Ní thuigeann an sáthach an scang,
nuair bhionn a bholg féin teann.*

'The man whose stomach is well-filled has
little sympathy with the wants of the hungry.'

—Irish Proverb

Seán rolled back the barn door, and the four of them were confronted with a long centre aisle with rows of horse stalls on either side. Despite the dust motes circling in the air and straw and sawdust strewn on the floor, the place was surprisingly neat. A large tack room held bridles and saddles of various sizes and other accessories of the horse trade. Another room held barrels, once filled with feed, but standing empty of their larder. A few forlorn bales of hay lined the back wall.

Nuala stood and breathed in the scent of oats and hay, still perceptible in the air. "What would it be like to have not one horse, but a stable full of horses? What a marvel this is!"

"You are a horsewoman, then?" Seán inquired.

"A wannabe. I've loved horses my whole life. Granda had a couple horses that we rode when we were weans. They were gone by the time I was a teenager."

"A presence is very strong in here," Moira broke in. "I think I'll wander the aisle a bit."

"Should we come too? Or would you rather be alone?" Deirdre asked.

"Give me a few minutes."

Moira moved off, leaving Nuala and Seán talking horses, but Deirdre stood outside the feed room door keeping an eye on Moira. She wasn't about to let anyone, spirit or otherwise, interfere with her sister again if she could help it. Her stomach began to clench in stress as she thought of Moira locked in the tower. She breathed deeply to regain calm.

About three-quarters of the way down the aisle Moira stopped in front of a stall and peered in. It seemed no different than any of the others, but something drew her to it, and she opened the stall door and went inside.

"This was her stall." A young man materialized next to her. His dark, wavy hair was cut short on the sides, with a wayward mop hanging over one blue-green eye. Freckles dotted his face and the beginning scruff of a beard sparsely covered his chin.

"A favourite of yours?" Moira coaxed.

"I knew you'd be able to hear me! When I saw you up in the tower, I finally felt some hope that I could reach someone. Do you see me as well?"

"Aye. Who are you?"

"I was called Paddy Mahoney, but no one has called me that in a long while."

"Talk to me, Paddy. Whose stall was this?"

"Queen Maeve. She was definitely feisty, like her namesake. But she and I got along just grand. She was a racer, and a good one."

"Who was her owner?"

"That would be Master Phillip McGuire."

"Phillip. Not John, then … When were you born, Paddy?" Moira's brain was racing trying to find her way in this tale without losing the teller.

"I don't exactly remember. I remember when I died, though!"

"Let's start there, then."

"It was 1848. I'd made it through the worst of the Hunger Times, so I thought I was doing alright. Ha!" His laugh sounded rueful.

"Are you Phillip's son?"

"Nah. His slave, more like. When Da, my sister, and older brothers died of the Hunger, Ma and my youngest brother were sent to the workhouse over in Naas near where we lived. That filthy place was practically in our backyard. Father Doyle got Mr. McGuire to hire me on here. At first, I was just an errand boy and mucked the stalls, but turned out I was pretty good with the horses. After a while, he let me lead horses down to the pasture and fetch them in at night. I worked for food—well, mostly I got stirabout—and an empty stall to sleep in."

"Not the greatest wages, but things were not so bad?"

"For a bit. Then Marcus started messing with me."

"And Marcus was …?"

"McGuire's oldest son. He didn't like me. Broderick liked me though. He was my age and we got along great. Marcus was jealous of my friendship with his brother, and the way I was able to calm Queen Maeve when no one else could. He was always trying to get his father's attention by getting me in trouble."

"What happened in 1848?"

"Moira, are you there? You've been gone for a while." Deirdre appeared at the stall door and Paddy was gone.

"Was just getting to the good part."

"Oh! You've made a connection."

"Well, he'll need a bit of coaxing, but he wants to tell

his story. He must think there is something we can do for him, though I can't imagine what, as he's been dead and gone for over a hundred years."

"I'm sorry I interrupted; do you think he'll come back?" Deirdre and Moira walked back to where Seán and Nuala were sitting on a couple of hay bales, their heads close together as they talked quietly. They jumped apart when the two entered the feed room.

"What's happened?" Nuala asked.

"Moira made contact."

"A young man named Paddy has been hanging out here for about 150 years. He's stuck about something that he needs help clearing so he can move on," Moira explained as she sat next to Nuala.

"I thought you said there were two presences in the tower," Seán said.

"We didn't get that far, but you're right. I'm sure Paddy is only part of the problem with your haunting."

"What do we do now?" Seán had begun pacing the small room.

"Well, I'd like to finish our tour of the house since we are already here. Then there is some research that would be helpful," Moira said.

"Research! I can help there. What kind of research?" Deidre asked.

"A couple things. We need to look into vital records and try to trace the Mahoney family from this area. I'd like to get some facts that corroborate Paddy's story."

"Let me do that," Nuala suggested. "I can get Ma to help me; genealogy is her area of expertise."

"Nuala's right, I'm no good at family history stuff. Anything else I can do?" Deirdre asked.

"I agree with Seán that we should trace the history of the estate owners. I have a few names and a possible timeframe now that might help there. Seán, will you move forward with that?"

"I'm on it."

"Deirdre, will you check the horseracing circuit back in the 1800s? The Curragh isn't far from here; see if a horse named Queen Maeve and her owner, Phillip McGuire, trained or raced there."

"This should be fun," Deirdre replied.

"*Phillip* McGuire … the estate has been in the McGuire family for several generations?" Seán had stopped pacing and turned to face Moira. "Generations of McGuires who have been tormenting the people around them."

"I don't have all the details yet, but you may be right."

Back at the house, they began a systematic check of the rooms on the ground floor: the morning room, sun lounge, billiards room, dining room, office/study, pantry/

larder and a large kitchen/breakfast room. They even ascended the second tower, but there was nothing unusual there—no hash marks or secret locks that they could see. They ended in the drawing room, where nothing seemed out of place though there were a lot of things: knickknacks, vases, paintings, lamps, tables.

"So much stuff!" Nuala exclaimed as she twirled in a circle, surveying the room. "Dusting everything would take several days."

"I know, it's a mess. I couldn't live with all this. If I decide to keep it, there will definitely be a huge estate sale." Seán sounded apologetic.

"*If* you decide to keep it? You must! It's class!" Nuala was now inspecting some figurines in a glass case. "But you're right, downsizing the contents would be a start. You could hold dances in this room if you got rid of most of the furnishings."

"I'm not much of a dancer."

Nuala looked at him but said nothing.

"I suppose I could give it a lash," he said, his face flushing red.

Deirdre laughed and grabbed Moira's arm, marching her out into the foyer.

"What d'ya think? Any new clues pop up for you?"

"Paddy seems to be laying low for the time being,

and I don't feel anything malevolent like I did in the tower earlier, so, I guess we can't do much more here."

"It's getting late; time we headed back," Nuala was saying to Seán as they joined Moira and Deirdre.

"As you wish," Seán replied.

They agreed to meet again at the estate the following Saturday, after they had a chance to do their research assignments. Moira suggested Nuala need not come up from Schull; she could email anything she and Ma could dig up on the Mahoney family.

"We'll see. I'll decide closer to next weekend. If things aren't too busy at the inn, I may as well join you here. It's all very exciting and I don't want to miss out on anything."

"I hope you decide to come," Seán said.

Nuala smiled.

~

As soon as the girls pulled away from the house, Deirdre said, "Well, it seems Nuala's got a new friend."

"Could be a bit more than that, I'd say," Moira chimed in.

But Nuala wouldn't take the bait. "You can say what you want; I think he's nice."

"Not a dancer, though." Deirdre refused to let up.

"But he comes with a haunted house; you can't beat that!" Moira laughed.

"Seriously, Moira, I was scared back there in the tower. What if something awful had happened?" Nuala said, changing the subject.

"A spirit's power is somewhat limited. I don't think I was ever in any real danger."

"Remember that time on the cliffs by St. Mary's?" Deirdre reminded her, "That was pretty scary, wasn't it?"

"Aye, but then Nana B came. She told me I would be protected; that I just had to call on the powers of good and I'd have support. I trust her. She hasn't steered me wrong yet. The more I'm involved with the world of spirits, the more I'm learning how to deal with it."

It was late when they arrived back at the flat. Nuala slept on her sisters' couch for the night to get an early start for home the next day.

∼

They awoke to a spitting rain and chill wind. "I'll be driving slower in this mess. We've got several bookings due to arrive this afternoon, so I should be there in time to help Ma," Nuala said as her sisters walked out to the truck with her after breakfast. "Let's check in with each other mid-week to see where we all stand on our assignments."

"Sounds good. Maybe you could be the one to check in with Seán for us, Nuala, if it's not too much trouble." Moira grinned as she hugged her sister goodbye.

"It's not too much trouble," Nuala said good-naturedly. "Slán agat."

"Slán abhaile."

"Love you, bye!" Deirdre waved from the door.

As the two watched their sister drive away, Moira commented, "She really has grown up."

"Not long ago our slagging would have brought tears. Definitely not as much fun anymore," Deirdre replied.

Chapter Twenty-Nine

Is do áibill fhásas breo.
'From a spark groweth a blaze.'
—Irish Proverb

"Heya, just checking in—it's midweek." The sound of Nuala's cheery voice greeted Moira as she tidied up after breakfast.

"You're sounding chipper; have you already spoken with Seán this week?"

"He called last night. And Tuesday night, and Monday night, and Sunday."

"Whaat? Guess he's trying to make up for all the months he's ignored you."

"Ha! Something like that. But I do like him; it's been fun getting to know him even if it's just over the phone."

"As Ma would say, 'faint heart never won fair lady.'"

"She did say that very thing, after his third night of calling."

"Well, what's the news? Has he made any discoveries? And what about the research into the Mahoney family?"

"Right; first the deed. We all worked together on it. Seán searched Griffith's Valuation and the Registry of Deeds, and Ma and I did some family history work on the McGuires as well as the Mahoneys. Philip McGuire was the first owner. He lived on the property for some years, I'm assuming in the cottage, before building the main house in 1844. After his death in 1868, the property continued in the family with his son, Marcus. Next owner was Marcus' son, Hugh. He was the one who transitioned the enterprise from horseracing to the stud farm and breeding operation. His son, William, inherited in 1935. That was John McGuire's father. John inherited in 1985 at the age of twenty-six."

"Thanks, Nuala, that sounds like it was a lot of work. What did you learn about the Mahoney family?"

"Ah. There was a Patrick—I'm assuming that's our Paddy—who was born in 1834 to Patrick Mahoney and Sally Keane. His baptismal record is in the Church of Our Lady and St. David, which is the closest Catholic Church near the Naas Workhouse."

"Good bit of detective work, Nuala. You must have

taken notes when I said Paddy told me his family's home was near the Naas Workhouse."

"Just doing my job." Nuala smiled. "Anyway, there are baptismal entries for Patrick, as I said, and two other boys, Brian and Joseph, born earlier—1830 and 1832—and then another son Peter in 1836. The last record is a daughter, Maureen, born in 1841. The burial records tell the rest of the story. The father, two older sons and Maureen all were buried in 1845-46. Nothing for the mother, Patrick or the younger son."

"Well, if the mother—you said her name was Sally?"

"Right."

"If she went to the workhouse, likely around 1845 or 1846 when the other family members died, she might be buried there. I don't know if they kept records of the deaths though. There was a burial ground attached to the workhouse."

"Ma and I can check that out, if you want. We'll call the Kildare County Library; they hold the workhouse records."

"That leaves young Peter. Let's find out if he died in the workhouse. Search the parish records about fifteen or twenty years forward for a marriage for him, in case he lived through the workhouse experience."

"Will do. Also, there's something odd I found in

the burial register. There's a footnote, not an actual burial record, stating that an unbaptised daughter, Betsy, born of Patrick and Sally Mahoney died in 1839, age one day."

"Huh. Back then the unbaptised weren't allowed burial within the churchyard. How sad."

"I thought so. When I read that, I had such an awful feeling. One more thing—the records indicated that the priest at the time was a Father Gerald Doyle. Didn't Paddy say his priest recommended him to McGuire?"

"Father Doyle! Good catch again. Not that I doubted him, but this lends credence to Paddy's story, for sure."

"What about the racehorse, Queen Maeve? Did Deirdre come up with anything there?"

"Let's see … here's her notes. I'd let her go over it with you but she's out for a run at the moment. Ah, here it is. In 1790, the Turf Club, now the Irish Horseracing Regulatory Board, published the first Irish Racing Calendar with details of the races. Deirdre was able to look at microfilmed copies of the Calendar for the years 1840 to 1850. As a three-year-old filly, Queen Maeve, owner Philip McGuire, was a favourite in 1846. She won in several categories in 1846, 1847, and 1848; after that, nothing. She seems to have dropped out of the racing scene altogether. In 1849, McGuire entered another horse, a colt named Reginald Star who did fairly well, but not as outstanding as Queen Maeve."

"According to Paddy, that's when she died, but we need to rule out the possibility she was pulled for breeding purposes. She'd be about the right age for a brood mare. I wonder if Seán has access to any of McGuire's breeding records?"

"I'll ask him next time we talk. I really hope Paddy appears this weekend, that would be a good question to ask him. We've got to know what happened in 1848!"

"You're right, another chat with Paddy is vital. Have you thought about coming back up here this weekend?" Moira asked.

"I shouldn't. We're booked for the next ten days. But let me work on it—I may have an idea that will allow me to come."

"Hmmm. More mysteries. Call me when you decide. Oh, and thank Ma for me for all that research."

"Well, I did most of it. Ma coached me a bit, but once I got started into the records, it was kinda fun. I can see why she loves it so much. And these aren't even my people. They seem to come alive when you read about their lives.

"And there's no mystery about this weekend. I'm thinking about asking my cooking partner from school, Molly Ronan, to fill in for me here for a few days. She's looking for a venue to practice some of her skills and said she envied me having a built-in practice site right at home. I need to see if she's available. I'll let you know soon."

Gail Grant Park

"Love you, bye," They both said, and laughed.

Chapter Thirty

*"Spectres hovered gloomily over the reedy
Marsh or the moor, or arrayed themselves
on the blasts of the wind; and pale ghosts,
messengers of the unseen world, brought back
the secrets of the grave."*

—Donald Ross of the Inverness Gaelic Society

"Thanks for coming up; I know it's a long drive for you. I'd come down to Schull to see you, but the ghosts are all up here." Seán took hold of Nuala's hand as they walked around the grounds of the estate, giving Moira some space for Paddy to appear. Nuala felt a little thrill go through her at his touch.

As they neared the treeline, they came across a patch of ground that was encircled with an iron rail fence. Approaching curiously, they discovered it was the McGuire Farm Cemetery containing about twenty headstones in various states of disrepair. They stooped to inspect each, brushing away lichen from the engravings.

"Look, Seán, here is a child's grave." Nuala read the inscription aloud, "'Baby Caroline, born April 23, 1857, died April 25, 1857. Rest with the Angels.' How sad."

"There's another here next to it: 'Liam McGuire born June 6, 1859 died June 10, 1859 You are loved.' Do you know who these graves are for?" Seán asked.

"I remember the main characters. Philip McGuire's son, Marcus took over the estate when his father died in 1868. He married a woman named Hannah something …"

"Here's a Hannah McGuire behind these two infant graves: 'born 1836 died June 7, 1859. Beloved Wife and Mother.' That seems easy enough to figure out. Hannah is the mother of these two children who died as infants, and then she died in childbirth with Liam."

"Here's Hugh's grave. He's the oldest son who inherited from Marcus in 1905. He died in 1935. Poor kid had to grow up without a mother, it seems. So much heartache for one family," Nuala said.

"These others all seem too crumbly and crusted over with lichen to read. Maybe we can work on cleaning them up and making this whole cemetery more presentable."

"That would be a worthy project if you are planning to keep the place. If not, you can let the new owners worry about it," Nuala said.

"Hmm ... definitely something to think about."

They walked on further, entering the wooded path through the trees.

"I'm trying to understand what your sister does ... er ... is doing. How did this all start, with the ghosts, I mean?"

"She's had this connection with the Otherworld ever since her childhood friend died in a car accident when they were weans. I guess Julia's visits opened the door, and Moira didn't know any better so accepted it as normal. Our nana visits her the most, helping her understand how the Otherworld works."

"That's deadly! I mean, don't you wish you could see the ghosts?"

"Well, I do sometimes, in my dreams," Nuala gave Seán a sideways glance to check how he accepted this bit of news. She didn't often share that part of herself with anyone.

"Dreams, huh?" Seán sounded sceptical. "That's not exactly the same thing, though, is it? Aren't our dreams a manifestation of our own subconscious?"

"Sometimes they are. But sometimes the veil between this world and the next is very thin. The dream state is a thin place, where we are more open and receptive to messages from those in the Otherworld."

"I don't know. I mostly dream about being naked in

public when I'm supposed to give a presentation, or being late for something, or forgetting which class I'm supposed to be in back in Senior Cycle." Seán laughed and continued, "Maybe you're reading too much into it."

Nuala disengaged her hand from Seán's. She didn't respond, but, looking straight ahead, quickened her pace until she'd put some distance between them.

"Hey, I didn't mean to upset you. I thought you were the normal one. You know, Moira with her ghosts, and Deirdre's some kind of yogi medicine woman with all her plants and herbs and stuff."

When Nuala didn't stop walking, he continued, "I'm making a right hames of it; I'm such a dope. Nuala, wait." He caught up with her and she turned to look at him.

"Just because you don't understand something, doesn't mean you should pooh-pooh it," Nuala said evenly.

"You're right. I want to understand. Tell me about your dreams."

But the closeness of the moment had passed and Nuala no longer felt comfortable sharing her inner world. She changed the subject. "Have you decided to keep the place, or are you still wanting to sell it?"

"It's sort of growing on me. I mean, I can do without the hauntings, but I believe I can make it a happier place to be than it has been from the sound of it."

"A happy place. Aye, I can see that."

As they walked back towards the house, Nuala was torn between wanting to see where this relationship might lead and already feeling that it was not meant to be.

~

Moira took her time wandering the length of the barn, stopping at several horse stalls, but there was no sign of Paddy. She was about to head back to the main house when she felt a presence and turned slowly to see Nana Brigid.

"Yes! Did you hear my heart hoping for help?"

"Something like that; I have come to give you a tool you may find useful in the coming days."

"A tool? What kind of tool?"

"Words; powerful words. Words that will protect you when you need protection most."

~

Having checked with Seán, Deirdre was tidying up the kitchen garden. She'd brought her gardening tools and had already cleaned out the dead debris and leaves from around the perennials. She loosened the soil in preparation for planting seeds: rue to bring light into the space and to ward off evil; Angelica as a powerful protector; sage for enlightenment—

"I thought I'd find you here," Moira said, "Where are Seán and Nuala?"

"They headed down to the wood about half-hour ago. Evidently there's a path that meanders through. Seán thinks it was used for hunting way back when. And you? Have you seen Paddy?"

"Naw, but he'll show up; I was thinking I'd spend some time down by the paddocks. He mentioned that was part of his job, to lead the horses there and back."

"Good luck. I'll be here if you need me." Deirdre went back to her task as Moira headed towards the pastureland.

Moira found a hospitable spot overlooking the paddocks, now overgrown with no grazing horses to keep them trimmed. She sat on a log, stretching out her legs. Her gaze took in the lush green fields criss-crossed by hedgerows and the occasional stone wall. Flocks of sheep grazed, dots of slow-moving white in the distance. Moira gave a deep sigh of contentment and closed her eyes.

"I'm here, Paddy, and ready to listen to the rest of your story, if you're ready to share it with me."

After a few moments, she felt a shiver of energy in the air coalesce in front of her. Paddy appeared with a huge grin on his face. "It's good to see you again, Moira."

"Aye, and yourself."

"I've sure been lonely with no one to talk to ... well, except Marcus, and he doesn't talk, he glowers ..."

"Tell me more about Marcus. Was he involved in what happened in 1848?"

"My death? Aye. You see, I told you I was good with Queen Maeve. She would let me get on her, bareback, and I'd ride her partway to and from the paddocks where no one could see us. Happiest times of my life. I felt so free. But it didn't last long. Marcus followed me, spying, and confronted me when I was on Queen Maeve. He grabbed her halter and told me I was in big trouble. Maeve didn't like that; she didn't like him. She reared up and threw me off, then took off for the woods at a gallop. There was no way either of us could catch her, she was so fast."

"Were you hurt badly?"

"Naw, but we had to go back to the house and tell McGuire that we'd lost Queen Maeve. Of course, Marcus put it all on me, nothing about him grabbing her halter and scaring her. McGuire ran to the barn and saddled up another horse and took off after her."

"Did he find her?"

"Aye, he found her alright. Seems there used to be a cottage out in the wood, abandoned since anyone could remember. Maeve ran across the old well there and broke through the rotted cover, breaking her leg in the process. Shortly after McGuire took off after her, we heard the gunshot."

"Go 'way! He had to put her down?"

"He was mad, he was. His prize filly, gone, and I was to blame. I was in the barn getting feed for the other horses when he returned. I didn't even see it coming. He hit me so hard I was lifted off my feet and hit my head on the metal rim of the grain barrel coming back down. Must've hit it just right; that's the last thing I remember until I was aware of looking down on my body at the bottom of the well."

"The same well Queen Maeve got hurt on?"

"Funny, right? Guess he thought it was fitting."

"I'm assuming then, that McGuire didn't report your death. Did no one come looking for you? Father Doyle, maybe?"

"Don't know. I didn't start hanging around here right away. Hard to tell … time, that is. We don't measure it the same way on this side. Dying is a bit disorienting …"

"Paddy, that would explain why you seem to be stuck here, why you haven't moved on. I think we need to find your bones and give you a proper burial."

"That would be grand. Maybe then I can finally get away from Marcus."

"Do you know why he is stuck here?"

"For a while, I thought it might be my fault."

"How's that?"

"Well, after I got done looking at my body lying at

the bottom of the well, I may have cursed him … some little thing about 'may his sleep be like the sleep of Foillen in the Castle of Naas …' but I decided I don't have that much influence over things and he's just angry all the time here, like he was in life.

"It wasn't too bad for a while, when I was here alone. It was kind of peaceful. Then he showed up and picked up where he left off; except he can't hurt me anymore. I get it. He was hurt a lot too."

"Tell me about that."

"His da, Mr McGuire, was a hard man; very strict with his sons. Any little thing they did wrong—even looking at him the wrong way—he'd make them spend the night in the tower room." Paddy gave a little shudder at the memory.

"You mean the room I got locked in last week?"

"When you were here last? That's the one. He made it special as a punishment room. I heard, but I don't know for sure, that he even locked Mrs. McGuire in there once."

"Go 'way!"

"And she wasn't the last. Another lady got put in there not too long ago; she was real nice, Miss Eveleen …"

Moira felt a shock go through her body. She tried to remain calm so as not to scare off Paddy as she said, "You saw Eveleen McGuire in the tower room?"

"The one who was here right before the place went empty. She seemed so sad; I tried to talk to her, but she couldn't hear me."

"I guess you would have seen quite a few things, hanging around here for over a century." *I can understand why Eveleen kept this from her son. It would definitely overshadow his ability to live in this place. Now it's up to me to tell him the truth.*

Moira could see Seán and Nuala coming out of the wood. Something seemed a bit off with their body language.

"Paddy, we are going to take care of this. We will give you the burial you deserve, in consecrated ground."

Dark clouds had been gathering for some time as they spoke, and now the skies opened with a lashing.

"Gotta leg it, Paddy, but I'll be back." Moira threw her jumper over her head and ran back to the house. She arrived at the same time as Seán and Nuala. Deirdre had prepared tea and they all sat in the kitchen drying off with towels she had at the ready.

"Seán, you've got a well-equipped kitchen here," Deirdre said as she passed around the cream and sugar. She'd also put out a plate of crisp sandwiches.

"I decided to hang out here for a bit, and bought a few things. I'm camped out in one of the upstairs bedrooms. Makes things easier until all this is settled. Hey, you all are welcome to stay here as well, for as long as you need. There's plenty of room." Seán included the three of them in the invitation, but he was looking at Nuala.

"Thanks for the offer, but we need to get back to Dublin and check on a few other things we've got going. But we'll be back. I learned quite a bit today." Moira filled them in on her visit with Paddy, but left out the detail of Nana Brigid's visit, keeping it close to her heart for the time being. And she didn't mention Paddy's revelation about Eveleen's imprisonment. Not yet. She'd have to find the right time and place.

"Did you and Nuala see anything that might be an old cottage, maybe a foundation or a well in the wood today?" Moira asked when she'd finished Paddy's tale.

"I didn't, but then, we weren't looking for it," Nuala said. "We did find the McGuire cemetery though."

"It's still rotten out there and getting dark, but I'll check it out tomorrow in daylight," Seán said.

"Well, watch yourself. If there is a well, even if McGuire put a new cover on it, by now it's most likely rotted again," Moira cautioned.

"Ha! Did anyone else just hear Ma's voice in their head saying, 'One look before is better than two behind?'" Nuala smiled for the first time since they all arrived back at the house.

Chapter Thirty-One

—

Ferr beagáu don ghaol na morándon aitheantas.

'Better a little relationship than much acquaintance.'

—Irish Proverb

"The weather a bit cool this evening between you and Seán?" Deirdre inquired after the sisters left Seán and the estate behind.

Nuala had been waiting for and dreading this moment, when her ever-attuned sisters would start in on what she was feeling and how things were going. "Ugh! I don't want to talk about it. He's such a goon!"

"Spill it, Nuala; we are here for you," Moira encouraged.

"Wait, did anything happen while you were in the woods? First kiss?" Deirdre asked.

"Quite the opposite. We're just so different. I don't

think it's going to work out. Maybe I was caught up in the idea of the estate, and horses, and having someone who thought I was special. Oh, let's not talk about it, please."

They rode in silence until Deirdre said, "You're not the kind of girl who falls in love with a guy for his money and horses."

"Thank you for saying so, and I do know that. I'm trying to rationalize how I got to this place." Nuala was happy that Deirdre pressed her to talk. She felt better already, getting it out and talking it through with her sisters, as she knew she would, eventually.

"Are you still planning to stay through Sunday?"

"I don't know. When I checked in with Molly earlier, she said things are going great and I should stay as long as I like, but … I don't know."

"That settles it; we're taking you out. Stay through Tuesday. There's a new band playing at the Gem Sessions this week. I've heard they're cracking," Deirdre coaxed.

"You've twisted my arm," Nuala laughed. And she did feel much better.

~

Voicemail again. Seán tossed his mobile on the bed and fell back onto the pillow. He'd been trying all Sunday to reach Nuala, to apologize again for being an eejit, but she wasn't taking his calls. When his mobile buzzed, he grabbed it and sat up, but saw it was his mate, Geoff.

"Howsagoin, Geoff?"

"How ya doing, mate? You still out at that monstrosity of yours?"

"It's complicated—" Seán began.

"Sure look, you need to have some fun, mate. You've been tied up with that place for ages. Come out with me for a few pints and we'll make a night of it."

"You know what? You're right. I'm outta here. Thanks, mate."

Seán packed a few things, and as he drove through the tree-lined entrance, he remembered he hadn't checked for the cottage ruins or an old well like he'd promised. He'd faffed around all Sunday worrying about how to make things right with Nuala. He'd definitely learned she was sensitive, especially about dreams. He'd have to look into that a bit more so he could talk to her about it intelligently—if she ever let him talk to her again.

~

"Nice crowd," Deirdre noted as the three girls made their way into the Gem Sessions and found seats. They'd arrived early enough to get settled before the actual concert began. Moira's casual glance at the crowd was arrested on one couple, seated across the room from them.

"Oh, boy. Don't look now, but is that Seán?" she said in a low voice.

Nuala did look and froze. It *was* Seán, sitting next to a dark-haired beauty. They were laughing at something and looked like a very happy couple. Nuala immediately pushed back her chair and headed for the entrance.

"Nuala, wait!" Deirdre called out. "Moira, stay here and save our seats; I'll go get her."

Deirdre found her sister pacing the sidewalk in front of the entrance.

"I am not going back in there! I knew he wasn't serious. It was all a joke to him. What a Gobshite! How did I fall for all that? I thought he liked me."

"Are you crying?" Deirdre pulled out tissue from her pocket.

"I'm too angry to cry. I want to go home. Please can we go?"

"Of course. Wait here, I'll go get Moira."

When Moira and Deirdre returned, Nuala said, "I'm so sorry. You should stay. I'll get a taxi back to your flat."

"That isn't going to happen," Moira said. "We'll all go."

Back at the flat, Moira and Deirdre pampered and fussed over Nuala, bringing her tea and toast and wrapping her in a quilt while they all dissected Seán's poor behaviour, which made Nuala feel much better.

"Oh, he's not that bad, you know," she finally confessed, laughing.

"There could be a good explanation," Moira suggested.

"Like what? That's his sister? Ha! We know that's not the case," Nuala said.

"Deirdre and I had planned to go back to the estate tomorrow. We set that up with Seán before we left on Saturday. Do you want to go with us, put off going home for another day? You can ask Seán himself what's going on," Deirdre asked.

"You know what? I'll do that. I want to hear what he's got to say."

"Fair play; I'm looking forward to that as well," Deirdre said.

~

"Seán!" Nuala sat bolt upright on the couch, cold sweat chilling her skin. Deirdre and Moira were soon at her side.

"What's wrong?" Moira said.

"I had a dream. I mean, a nightmare. I only hope it's not a precognition, or vision."

"Tell us." Deirdre sat next to Nuala and took her hand in her own; it was sweaty and shaking.

"I was following Seán at the estate. It was dark, and he had a green glowing light. He didn't know I was there. It was like he was in a trance. I followed him into the wood—it seemed we were going forever, but then he stopped near a large yew tree. I tried to call out to him, but I had no voice. Then he moved forward and disappeared. Poof! He was gone. Oh, I just know something is wrong. Something has happened, or will happen; it's bad."

"It's only six, too early to call him? That would ease your mind," Deirdre suggested.

"Right, it's not too early." Nuala rang Seán's number, but he didn't answer, which made her all the more worried.

"Well, let's get ready and head over there. We'll soon find out if there's a problem," Moira said.

In a little over an hour, they'd arrived at the estate, and though Seán's car was parked out front, he didn't come out to greet them as usual. Deirdre walked up to the door and knocked. They all waited a few moments, but when there was no response, Nuala tried the door.

It opened.

"Seán? Anyone here?" Moira called out as the girls stood tentatively in the foyer.

"What if he's hurt? What if that mean ghost, Marcus, has done something to him?" Nuala was starting to panic.

"Let's not get worked up just yet. Let's look around.

Umm, someone want to take the basement?" Deirdre asked.

"Let's stay together," Moira said.

After a thorough search of the house, they headed for the stables, but there was nothing to indicate Seán had been there.

"The woods. I know he's in the woods; he's hurt." Nuala turned and started out at a run for the path she and Seán had taken a few days earlier.

"Hey, Nuala, wait up! We're all in this together, remember?" Deirdre and Moira caught up with her on the path. As they went deeper into the wood, Deirdre said, "Does this look anything like your dream? Do you think the yew tree was a real tree? Could you find it again?"

"The yew tree is symbolic of death and dying, so it might only be representative of Nuala's fears," Moira said.

"Great, that doesn't help, Moira," Nuala said. "I don't think we were on the path for long. It seemed like there were brush and brambles I had to step over and branches to push aside."

They'd gone a bit further on the path when Nuala said, "Here, look—there's some broken branches, like someone stepped off the path."

They followed the makeshift path for a few yards when Nuala stopped, causing Moira to bump into her from behind.

"That tree! Well, it's not a yew … is it an oak? But this looks like the place where I saw Seán disappear." Looking around the area, they saw what appeared to be a foundation of loose stones. The day had started out cloudless, but as they headed towards the large tree, a dark mist rose up, the temperature dropped sharply, and a fierce wind blew so hard they could barely stand up.

"This is not normal," Deirdre shouted to be heard over the roaring wind. "What's happening?"

"I think we've stirred up the ghost of Marcus. He evidently doesn't want us here. That means we're in the right place," Moira called out. "Stand behind me. I've got this."

Nuala and Deirdre huddled near Moira as she raised her hands up high above her head. Then she spoke the words she'd learned from her grandmother's visit.

"In the name of the Divine One, I release you to the angels, never to return, never to be replaced. Angels of Light, I call upon you to escort this troubled spirit from this realm to a place of learning where he may develop goodwill towards all, the living and the dead."

The air seemed to shudder, and then the dark mist lifted and the wind calmed as quickly as it had begun.

Chapter Thirty-Two

Tar éis a chitear gach beart.
'It is afterwards events are understood.'
—Irish Proverb

"What just happened? What was that? You alright?" Deirdre looked incredulously at Moira, who had slumped to the ground.

"I'm grand. More than grand. 'Powerful words.' That's what Nana Brigid said a few days ago when she taught them to me and told me I would soon need them. I had no idea at the time what that meant."

"A few days ago? Why didn't you tell us?" Nuala said.

"I don't know … they seemed somehow … sacred? Not secret, so much as not to be shared lightly? I was holding them close for a while …"

A low moan interrupted them, and Nuala turned toward what she now saw was a jagged piece of rotted wood jutting out from a hole in the ground.

"Seán!"

"Take care, Nuala, it could be dangerous," Moira said.

"Of course, it's dangerous, it's an old well! Seán has fallen in! Help me!" The three of them pulled away several pieces of the rotted cover and looked in. Seán lay in a crumpled heap about twenty metres down at the bottom of the well. His right leg was bent at an odd angle.

"Seán, I'm here! We'll get help! Hold on!" Nuala already had her mobile out and was dialling 999.

Another miraculous occurrence was that she had a phone signal in the woods. While Nuala stayed with Seán, Deirdre and Moira ran back to the house, stationing themselves at the end of the drive and by the path to direct emergency personnel. To Nuala it seemed like ages, but they arrived with the equipment needed to haul Seán safely out.

Seán could barely speak, slipping in and out of consciousness from the intense pain, but after a shot of painkillers he managed, "How did you find me?"

"I saw you and this place in a dream this morning. We came straight away and were able to find you. What were you doing out here? And when?"

"We've got to get him to hospital, ma'am," one EMT said as he and another hoisted Seán's stretcher between them and began moving as quickly as possible through the trees to the path where the vehicle was waiting.

"Can I ride with him to hospital?" Nuala asked.

"Are you a relative?"

"Um …"

"You can follow us in your vehicle. That would be best."

"Fine. Seán, is there anyone you'd like us to notify? Your girlfriend, perhaps?"

Seán looked at her quizzically, but said, "No …"

"I'll see you soon, then," Nuala said as they shut the ambulance doors.

As the three sisters sat in the hospital lounge, waiting for news, they discussed the events of the morning.

"Well so much for your theory that ghosts can't hurt people. Tell that to Seán when he gets out of surgery," Nuala said.

"I was wrong. But again, we received help from beyond in time to avert something worse. Your dream saved him, Nuala, and I agree that the ancestors sent it to you for Seán's sake," Moira said.

Hours later, the surgeon came out to where the girls had been waiting, not so patiently. Nuala jumped up from her seat and met him.

"How is he, Doctor?"

"He's still in Recovery, a bit groggy from the

anaesthesia. You can see him in about a half-hour. We set his leg, which was broken in two places. He's got a couple cracked ribs and a broken clavicle, which caused tremendous pain, I'm sure. He didn't lose much blood, which was helpful, but if he'd stayed there in that condition much longer, shock and hypothermia might have done him in."

Nuala's legs felt a bit wobbly and she sat down again. "Did he say how long he was out there?"

"It seems he fell about four this morning, so he was out there a good five hours."

"I had my dream right after that …"

"What was that?"

"Oh, nothing. Thank you, Doctor! Thank you so much!"

After the doctor left them, Deirdre said, "You should go in and see him on your own; we'll wait out here. Too many people …"

Nuala sent her a silent 'thank-you.'

~

"Hey," Seán managed when he saw her enter his room.

"Hey. How are you feeling?"

"Like a right jammy bloke. I thought I was a goner out there, at least when I was aware enough to realize anything."

"What were you doing out there, anyway?"

"I got home around three this morning. I was upstairs about to get to bed when I saw a light bobbing in the back, moving towards the wood. With the full moon I thought I could see fairly well, but I couldn't see a person, only this greenish glowing blob."

"I thought you had a flashlight."

"There wasn't one handy and I didn't want to let the intruder get out of my sight. I legged it after him. It was hard to keep up, I could never quite catch him, but if I slowed down, the light seemed to slow down too, like he was waiting for me. Anyway, shortly down the path he veered off into the brush, but I kept on. We came to some old clearing, with a few small trees, and it stopped and hovered in front of a big tree. I approached carefully, but I guess I was looking at the light and not at my feet, because, well, you know. I fell into that hole."

"It's a well that belonged to a cottage there. Only a few stones are left of the foundation. Seán, you could have been killed!"

"Don't I know it. And if you say that you found me because of a dream, then I am a full-fledged believer." He paused for a minute and a puzzled look came across his features. "Um ... as I was being loaded into the ambulance back there, you said something ...?"

"I asked about your girlfriend."

"That's it. I thought I was hallucinating. Why did you say that? What did you mean?"

"I mean yer wan from the concert last night."

"My—" Then the light dawned and he said, "Ah! You were at the Gem Sessions? You should have come over!"

"You were looking rather cosy; I didn't want to interrupt."

"Nuala, she is not my girl. I was there with my mate, Geoff and *his* girl. You must have seen us when Geoff was off in the jacks. I've known Geoff and Liz forever—they are mates from way back. Um, I was starting to hope *you* would be my girl …"

She moved closer to his bedside and planted a kiss on his forehead.

"I'm sorry for the awful things I was thinking—and saying to my sisters—about you."

"The misunderstanding was totally worth it." He grinned.

"Oh, here, I almost forgot." Nuala took an amber dropper-bottle of liquid out of her handbag. "This is Ma's boneset tincture. Probably wise not to let the staff see it, as I don't know that they are into alternative medicines here."

"And this will cure me? Grand!"

"Well, as Ma would say, 'the herb that is not got is

the one that cures,' but this will be a close second."

"And do I chuff it down in one go, or parse it out?"

"A couple droppersful three times a day should do it."

"Thanks a million, Nuala."

"You can thank Deirdre. She grabbed a bunch of her tinctures when we rushed out to find you after my dream. She also brought meadowsweet for when you're ready to get off the prescription painkillers."

He gazed at her with such soft eyes that she had to turn away. "Well, we'd better be off and let you rest. Did they say how long you'll need to be in hospital?"

"As soon as I can make arrangements for someone to come in and help out with things. I'm not going to be able to do much for myself for a while."

"Hmm …" Nuala's thoughts were percolating. She was about to say goodbye when Moira poked her head in.

"Mind if I join you for a minute? I have something I need to say to Seán," she said.

"Not at all, come in. Thank you for being here and for rescuing me," Seán said, motioning to the chair on the other side of the bed from where Nuala sat.

"It was Nuala's dream that saved you, but I'm sure she's told you that. Seán, I need to tell you something that I should have told you before now." Her serious tone had both Seán's and Nuala's full attention.

Moira took a deep breath and let it out slowly before speaking. "Last weekend when we were at the estate—the last time Paddy visited me—he told me something that I have been holding back from you, and I know it's something you need to know. Paddy saw your mother, Eveleen; he even referred to her by name."

"That makes sense, if he's been hanging around here for a hundred years, he's bound to have seen all the people who have lived here—"

"He saw her in the tower."

When neither Seán nor Nuala responded, just looked at her blankly, she continued in a rush to finish, "he said she was locked in there, her husband's prisoner. He didn't say how often or for how long, only that he felt sorry for her, she seemed so sad. I'm not sure why I didn't tell you sooner, I guess I was worried how you would take it; if you could live in that place knowing the extend of what she endured."

While Moira was speaking, Nuala had quietly taken hold of Seán's hand as it rested on the bed covers. Seán now looked at Nuala and squeezed her hand. Then he turned to Moira and said, "Thank-you for telling me. When we were in the tower, I had a strange feeling. I think I knew then that Eveleen had been there and not willingly. I'm not saying I felt her presence, I have no idea what that would even feel like, but I felt ... sad, and a sense of relief at the same time. Like she was no longer in that situation and she was happy. I certainly don't blame the house for what was done in it. I lay that all at the feet of McGuire."

Moira relaxed, glad she had shared the 'secret" and that Seán had received it with such grace. They visited a few more minutes, then the sisters rose to leave. Moira said goodbye and left Nuala to take her leave in private. When they were alone, Nuala leaned over and kissed Seán goodbye, this time on his cheek, and hurried out to join her sisters.

"How's he doing?" Deirdre asked.

"Grand. Well, as grand as can be expected seeing as it's a miracle he is still alive." Nuala filled them in on the details she'd learned of his fall, and the misunderstanding of the non-girlfriend.

"You must have seen the whole thing in your dream soon after it happened," Moira said.

"I got a few details wrong, but it definitely was a divine intervention that got us to him as quickly as we did. So, here's the thing: when Seán is released from here, he's going to need a lot of help for a while. I was thinking ... do you think Ma would let him stay at the inn for his recovery? Ma and I would both be there to help and—"

"And it would save you a lot of driving back and forth

for quite some time," Deirdre finished for her.

"Well, there's that, too." Nuala smiled.

"I like it, and I'm sure Ma will too. Here's another thing. I think someone should be checking on the estate until things are sorted out there. Maybe one or both of us"—here Deirdre looked at Moira—"could keep an eye on things until Seán is back on his feet."

"Here we are planning someone else's life, just like the good ol' days!" Moira laughed. "Let's check with Ma, then pass it by Seán before we get too ahead of ourselves."

The sisters headed back to the flat to regroup and get some proper nourishment other than vending machine fare. They had some work to do to put their plans in place.

Chapter Thirty-Three

Dearbhráthair don bhás an cod-ladh.
'Sleep is brother to Death.'
—Irish Proverb

Even though it was way past noon, Nuala prepared a full Irish fry up: sausage, tomatoes, eggs, beans, mushrooms and boxty. "What's the next step?" she asked as she handed plates to her sisters.

They had filled Dymphna in on the recent events and she was delighted with the proposed arrangement for Seán to come to the inn. Nuala called Seán and explained the plan to him, to which he also agreed with much enthusiasm. He told her where they could find a spare key to the estate for Moira and Deirdre to check on things there while he was gone. Nuala would head home in the morning, picking up Seán on the way. As exciting as that prospect was, she still felt left out as she thought of Moira and Deirdre continuing the investigation at the estate without her.

"Bones," Moira said. "We go back to the well and find a way to get down there safely to look for Paddy's remains."

"We'll need a long ladder. Maybe some kind of rope ladder. And a satchel for bringing up anything we may find. Trowels? Brushes? We don't want to damage anything." Deirdre started a list on a pad of paper at the kitchen table.

"Hold up. Should we be doing this on our own or is it time to call in authorities?" Moira worried.

"What authorities? The bones are ancient. There's no recent crime to report. 'Attempted murder by ghostly presence' is not going to set well with the gardaí, no matter how often they've let us work with them recently," Deirdre reminded her.

"True, but we can't just dig up human bones. We'll have to notify authorities if we do find something. The real question is, what reason do we give for being down in the well in the first place?"

"I know!" Nuala spoke up. "While I was talking to Seán, he mentioned that he didn't see his wallet when they gave him his personal stuff after surgery. You can go and look for whatever may have fallen out of his pocket when he was in the well."

"That's perfect. Then if we do find bones, we'll stop

and report it. It's a good thing Seán cancelled his contract with the estate agent and took the place off the market. We wouldn't want any interruptions," Deirdre said.

"Correction: *when* we find bones. But you're right; that's as good a reason as any for returning to the well," Moira said. "I promised Paddy he'd be buried properly in consecrated ground. We can talk to the parish priest in Naas. It would be grand if he could be put to rest with the other members of his family."

"What about the cemetery there on the property? Couldn't we bury his bones there? It's Seán's land, I'm sure he'll give permission," Nuala suggested.

"I'll see what Paddy thinks. But one step at a time. We don't even have any bones yet. I believe they are there in that well, but we won't know for sure until we look," Moira said.

~

In the morning, after seeing Nuala off, they made a quick stop at the hardware store for supplies. Equipped with a rope ladder, trowel, and backpack, they arrived in Kildare in the early afternoon. Once at the site, they decided Moira should stay above ground first, while Deirdre descended into the well. She carried the trowel in her backpack and wore a heavy-duty pair of gloves.

They fastened the ladder to the oak tree north of the well and Deirdre tested it several times before she was satisfied it would hold. The ladder fell about a metre short of the bottom, but it was an easy drop. Right away Deirdre saw Seán's wallet.

"First objective attained," she called up to Moira, who was peering over the edge. "It's fairly dry down here; not a lot of leaf mould or debris. I guess the well cover held up for most of the years. The layer of dirt at the bottom is soft, not super compacted. I'm sure that cushioned Seán's fall."

She began to dig with her trowel, heaping up shovelfuls along the edges of the well.

"I found somethi—ugh! It's a dead animal; I think it's a rabbit. I hope we don't have to sift through a lot of animal bones to find something human."

"I know we used it to dispose of animal carcasses on occasion." Paddy's voice made Moira jump. She turned to see him peering over her shoulder into the well.

"Paddy! Glad you could be here!"

"This place was empty back in my day too; I think they never were able to reach water in this well."

They watched Deirdre toil in silence for a few minutes, then Moira said, "When we find your bones, how would you feel about being buried here on the estate in the family cemetery? I know you weren't treated well here, and your family is buried elsewhere—"

"I may not have moved on to what's next, but I do know it doesn't matter where your bones lie. Marcus is buried in yon cemetery and he's still lingering here same as me. Although I haven't seen him lately … Anyway, I think it's more about acceptance and knowing someone has heard your story; knows you existed and what happened to you. Finding peace, ya know? You've already done that for me."

"It's not important to you to be buried with your family?" Moira pressed.

"And where would that be? In the poorhouse mass grave with Ma, or in the hedgerow outside the churchyard with Betsy? Naw. It don't matter. Whatever you want to do."

"If you were buried here on the property, it would be easier to mark your grave with a proper headstone, no questions asked."

"Eureka!" echoed from the bottom of the well.

"You found something?" Moira called down.

"Looks like a femur. Definitely human."

"Ayup. That's me alright," Paddy confirmed.

"Nice one, Deirdre. That's all we need. Come on up."

Chapter Thirty-Four

Éist le comhairle ó gach aon, agus déan do chomhairle féin.
'Listen to everyone's advice, but follow your own.'
—Irish Proverb

It was a bit more complicated than they expected. After notifying the gardaí of their find, a team was sent out immediately and the area was cordoned off. They unearthed a complete human skeleton, which they labelled, bagged and sent to a laboratory in Dublin.

And then the waiting began.

Deirdre called the lab every day. Moira called the gardaí every day. They always got the same message: "These things take time."

Meanwhile, Nuala called to update her sisters on her research into the Mahoney family.

"It took a while, but we've put together a family tree

from the church records showing descendants. Peter *did* survive the poorhouse and married in 1860. Ma and I traced his children and their children, looking for family members that may have stayed in the local parish. Four generations from Peter we've found that a Robert Mahoney still lives in Naas. We're hoping it's "our" Robert, and that would make Paddy his second great-granduncle."

"Bang on! Have you contacted him?" Moira asked.

"I wanted to check with you first, and see if you wanted to try to meet up with him in person. This is pretty intense stuff to hand to someone over the phone."

"You're right, you're right. That would be a better idea. Send me the details and Deirdre and I'll go over there. Oh, I hope he'll give us a DNA sample."

In the background, Nuala could hear Deidre say, "Ask her how Seán is doing."

"How is Seán doing?"

"He's grand. He's still on some meds, but getting off the painkillers. Tell Deirdre the meadowsweet is working wonders. I think he's enjoying all the attention from Ma. She's giving him the royal treatment."

"And how are you two getting on?"

"We're getting on." Nuala didn't elaborate, knowing Moira wouldn't dig any deeper.

"That's grand! We'll watch for your email with the

information on Robert. Thanks a million, Nuala, you're the best!"

"You heard all that?" Moira asked.

Deirdre nodded, "What should our approach be to this 'Robert?'"

"I'm not sure. It's going to take some delicate handling. It's a pretty fantastic story; out of the reach of someone not used to dealing with this kind of thing. I'm worried we won't get past the 'based on clues we got from your great-great-granduncle's ghost, we've dug up some bones and want to be sure they're his. Could you spit in this vial and we'll compare your DNA?'"

"That might not go over too well. What about if we go the workhouse route?" Deirdre suggested.

"What do you mean?"

"We could say that we are doing some research that includes the Naas Workhouse and are checking with locals who may have had ancestors who went there."

"Few people want to talk about that, but I can't think of anything better."

"It's just to get us in the door. Once we get talking, we can manoeuvre the conversation to the McGuires and the role they played in the Mahoney family. We can see if he has any knowledge of Paddy and the family history."

"And if he doesn't? Not everyone's family has a Ma

who eats and drinks genealogy."

"We can only try and see what happens."

~

The next day, armed with the family history Dymphna and Nuala had unearthed and Robert's address in Naas, the two sisters knocked at the door of a detached brick home on Kilcullen Road.

"May I help you?" A woman of about fifty stood in the doorway with a rolling pin in her hand and a toddler on her hip.

"Sorry to disturb you, is this the home of Robert Mahoney?" Deirdre asked.

"I'm Juliette Mahoney; my husband is out back. What is this about?"

"I'm Deirdre Gallagher, and this is my sister, Moira. We are doing some research on the history of this area and wanted to talk to your husband about his family. They've lived in Naas for some generations, have they not?"

"Come in, I'm sure he'll love to talk with you. He is a right history buff. Don't get him started on the Great Hunger; he'll talk your ear off."

She led the girls through a neat front room, kitchen, and a back door to the garden where a tall, slender man was on his knees turning over soil in a garden bed. He stood up as they approached.

"Rob, these young ladies want to talk to you about family history. Deirdre and Moira …"

"Gallagher," Moira supplied as she reached out her hand.

"Robert Mahoney, but I won't shake yer hand, covered in dirt as I am."

"Well, I'll leave you to it, there's more baking to do and Patrice still needs her lunch." Juliette returned to the house and Robert directed the girls to some chairs set out on the flagstone.

"That's our granddaughter. We have her weekday mornings while our daughter is at work. How can I help you?"

"You know a bit about your family history?" Moira began.

"Aye, Mahoney's have worked the soil here for generations. Gotten smaller and smaller until I'm here with my backyard patch of a garden, but there was a time …"

"Are you a descendant of Peter and Bernadette Mahoney?" Deirdre had pulled out her notebook and looked at the page.

"How do you know that?" He asked, with a note of suspicion in his voice.

"We're working on a project that involves the Naas

Workhouse during the Great Hunger. Records indicate that Peter was once a resident at the Workhouse. We were hoping you could tell us more about that time," Deirdre explained.

"I guess it's all a matter of public record. I don't mind talking about it. But that place! A disgrace to humanity. Man's inhumanity to man, so it was."

"Aye, it was," Deirdre agreed.

Juliette appeared then with an assortment of soft drinks, glasses, and a plate of biscuits. "I warned you not to get him started on that subject," she laughed. They thanked her for the refreshment and she returned to the house.

"Did Peter's mother die in the workhouse?" Moira probed.

"Well, nothing is written down. Family traditions tell the tale. We still don't know where the residents who died in there were buried. No markers. No records. But Sally never made it out alive, we do know that."

"And Peter?"

"Peter was just a lad; was there almost a year when his uncle found him and got him out. Sally was gone by then. Not a trace, just that she had died. Peter was raised by his uncle who had moved into the Mahoney cottage and taken over the farm for his brother when he learned he had died."

"Do your family traditions make mention of Paddy—or Patrick? He was a brother to Peter?"

"Paddy! Now that's the great mystery, isn't it?"

"What do you know about him?" Moira continued.

"Disappeared as well. Ended up like his ma, we guess. Went off to work as a stable hand for one of the local landowners and was never heard from again."

"Which landowner?" Deirdre asked.

"Philip McGuire."

Deirdre and Moira looked at each other with wide eyes. *Now what?* they silently communicated to one another. Then Deirdre said, "Robert, we may have discovered the answer to that mystery."

"What do you mean?"

"Are you aware that the last McGuire descendant recently died?"

"Read about that accident in the papers a while back. Car crash, a little over a year ago, wasn't it?"

"That's right. We are friends with the young man who inherited the McGuire estate through his mother, Eveleen McGuire—"

"Read about that too. All the best to him, I say."

"That's very kind of you. Anyway, Seán, the new owner, recently had an accident; he fell into an old unused well on the property."

"That's terrible! Is he okay?"

"He got hurt pretty bad, but in the process, old bones were discovered in the well; human bones from some time ago."

There was silence among the three as the girls let that sink in. Robert looked shocked, then puzzled, then questioned, "What does that have to do with me? Are you saying you think the bones belong to Patrick Mahoney?"

"Robert, as part of the McGuire history, we had also heard about Patrick's time there and his mysterious disappearance. Could it not be possible that he fell into the well, back so long ago?"

"Well, I suppose, it's possible. What do we do now?"

"The bones are being tested for age, gender, means of death, that sort of thing. They will also do DNA testing on them. We were hoping you would supply a DNA sample that could be compared to the bones. It's not going to give a definitive answer, only a percentage match that far back. But it will tell us if there is a relationship, and could solve your family mystery," Deirdre explained.

"I'll do it. Well, I should talk to my wife first … actually, it's *my* family; I want to know. How do I give a sample?"

They set Robert up with a DNA kit and gave him the address of the laboratory in Dublin where he should send it. They promised to keep him informed about the investigation and testing. He walked them through the house to the front door. As they passed through the kitchen, they said their goodbyes to Juliette and thanked her once again, grateful they were leaving Robert to explain their conversation.

Chapter Thirty-Five

—

*Is ionann seanfhocal agus cogar
gaoise onár sinsir.*
'A proverb is like a whisper from our ancestors.'
—Irish Proverb

After that, things moved quickly. Within a few days, Robert got a report back from the lab with his results. Soon after *that*, he got a visit from the gardaí investigating the bones.

"We understand Moira Gallagher discovered a relationship between you and the deceased," Garda John O'Rourke began.

"She and her sister are investigators. They traced my family history and knew about my great-great-granduncle Patrick, who used to work at the McGuire estate."

"You confirm that you have a relationship to someone who disappeared there a number of years ago?"

"Donkeys years! That would have been in 1848 or '49. Like I said, he was my great-great-grandfather's brother. There was no family around to check on him, but my great-great-grandfather, Peter Mahoney, could find no trace of him a few years later when he was able to look."

"You've seen the DNA report. Has it been explained to you?"

"I spoke with someone at the lab and they did explain." Robert pulled out the pages from the envelope. "It says here that I have a 3.125 shared percentage DNA with the bones that were found at the former McGuire estate. They explained that is equivalent to first cousins twice removed, or second cousins, or a second great-granduncle. Which is what I'm telling you is my relationship to Paddy Mahoney, who disappeared there over a century ago. The other number here is something called a centimorgan. Not sure what that means, but I've got 212.5 of those."

"Very good, sir. We thank you for your help in sending in the DNA sample. It certainly gives us a theory to work on as to how the bones got where they were."

"One thing the lab didn't tell me is anything about the bones themselves. Were they able to identify anything from them other than the DNA match?"

"Well, as you are the nearest of kin so far as we can determine, I can tell you that the bones belong to a

Caucasian male, between thirteen and sixteen years of age. They were dated to be from the time period you say your family last heard from Patrick Mahoney. They contained several broken bones, but it can't be determined if they were broken before the fall into the well, or after death. The skull was fractured from a sharp-force trauma, which was most likely the cause of death. I am sorry for your loss, sir."

"Thanks a million, but we lost him over one hundred and fifty years ago, so we did. What happens to him now?"

"The young woman, Deirdre Gallagher, has put in an official request for custody of the bones. As she and her sister discovered them, and as they are representing the property owner, who cannot be present at this time, they will be turned over to her in a matter of days. She has indicated that they plan to bury them in a cemetery."

"Fine. That's fine. Thank you for coming." Robert saw them out and immediately called Deirdre.

"Robert! How are you?" Deirdre answered the phone when she saw the caller ID.

"Gardaí just left; said you will be getting custody of Patrick's bones?"

"In a few days, they said. I was going to ring you to talk about it. Do you have any thoughts on what you would like to have happen?"

"Well, give him a decent burial, is all."

"There are options. Are you a member of a parish church where you would like him buried? Perhaps where his siblings and father are buried at Our Lady and St. David's? It would be up to you to explain the situation to the parish priest, and ask for the proper permissions and all …"

"Hmm. You said there were options. What other options?"

"Seán Kennedy, the new owner of the McGuire estate, has offered the family cemetery on the property for Patrick's burial. It could use a bit of cleaning up and tidying after being neglected for so long—alright, it's in a desperate state. But we plan to get started on it right away, in respect for the dead, even if you don't want Patrick there."

"That sounds nice. And maybe even Juliette and I could lend a hand with the clean-up. Our family has always been a bit reserved, not showy, if you know what I mean. I'm not keen on making a circus of this in the parish, you know?"

"I do. Let's plan on a small rite of committal at the McGuire family cemetery. Do you know of anyone who could do that? Any men of the cloth in your acquaintance?"

"Let me think on it. It's possible …"

"Grand! We'll talk soon."

Chapter Thirty-Six

"The most important things in the world are to get something to eat, something to drink and somebody to love you."

—Brendan Behan

The simple, granite headstone read: 'Patrick Mahoney, b. 1834—d. 1848. Rest in Peace.'

"The place sure looks grand. And I see you discovered my birthday!"

"Hiya Paddy. Haven't seen you in a while. I imagine having your bones moved around and poked and prodded might cause you to keep a low profile." Moira was waiting by the cemetery entrance for the Mahoneys to arrive. Robert and Juliette were bringing Juliette's cousin, Father James McDougal, who would pronounce the Rite of Committal and bless Patrick's grave.

"Any last words before the crowd gathers?" Moira

asked. "Seán and Nuala couldn't make it, but Deirdre will be out shortly. She's inside getting a few things set up for your wake—food and drink for your family after the ceremony."

"My family! Sounds grand. And I get a wake as well? Moira you are a sound lass!"

Moira laughed. "It's been grand to know you, Paddy. I'm grateful for the adventure. But what have you been up to while your bones have been off with the experts?"

"Busy, busy. I have moved on somewhat and I tell you, I'm learning a lot. This might be my last chance to visit, seeing as it's my burial and all, but I had to say 'thank you' and let you know that everything is grand–more than grand. I've seen Ma and Da, and even my little sis, Betsy, is here. She may not have been buried in the churchyard, but ya know what? She didn't need to be. I found out that *all* little ones who die go directly to heaven. They are pure and innocent. They don't even have anything to feel bad about or repent, so they don't need baptism. All that grieving and worrying Ma did and it wasn't even necessary."

"Well, the heavens sure seem like they're smiling now; this is the first sun we've seen all week. A grand aul day for a burial, don't you think?"

But she was alone, as she watched Deirdre leading a group of people down the path towards her. Not only

Robert, Juliette, and her priestly brother had come, but the Mahoneys' two children and five grandchildren were all there as well. *Indeed, it is a grand aul day for a burial.*

Book Four
We Are Dreamers

(Is brionglóidí muid)

Chapter Thirty-Seven

At all Hallows Tide, may God keep you safe
From goblin and pooka and black-hearted stranger,
From harm of the water and hurt of the fire,
From thorns of the bramble, from all other danger,
From Will O' The Wisp haunting the mire;
From stumbles and tumbles
and tricksters to vex you,
May God in His mercy, this week protect you.

—Irish Blessing for Samhain

October 4, 2010, Ballydehob, Ireland

"I was really flying this time!" Nuala enthused, her soft chestnut hair brushing her cheek. "Not the pumping-my-arms-as-hard-as-I-can-to-barely-stay-aloft kind of flying, but effortlessly soaring through the air!"

"I love flying dreams," sighed sixteen-year-old Fiona. "Well, I'm sure I *would* love them, if I ever could have one."

"Attention everyone! I appreciate all your energy

and excitement to begin, but let's have a quick summary of what dreamwork is all about, as there are a few newbies here tonight." Shelagh, aka Silverstar Moonbeam, looked around the candlelit room of about a dozen dreamers. It had only taken a few touches after closing—some mood lighting, a bit of incense and imagination—to magically transform the café into this Cave of Dreams. In a similar way she, too, was transformed, from shy, unassuming waitress by day to a dynamic and influential Dream Leader here among her followers.

She spoke softly but firmly as she began setting the ground rules for the next ninety minutes:

"We'll be partnering up in twos, taking turns sharing our dreams. The listener will ask questions to elicit a more complete picture of the dream. Sometimes it helps to pretend the listener is from another planet—for instance, you can say, 'Describe the elephant. What is an elephant like to you? Is it huge and frightening? Or, is it a gentle giant, nurturing and never forgetting?'

"You can ask if there is anyone or anyplace in waking life that reminds you of the dream elements. Once the dreamer has recounted the dream, you can refer to the suggested questions in your handout.

"Remember, you must not try to interpret the dream for someone else. Begin your comments with, 'If this were my dream.' In this way, you may be able to open up possibilities of interpretation for the dreamer without imposing your symbolism on them. It is ultimately their own interpretation that will have meaning.

"Let us now open the space for our energy work." Shelagh sat cross-legged on the floor and with closed eyes, intoned, *"We invite our allies, spirit animals, ancestral and angelic guides to be present and interact with us for the greater good of all."*

She looked up and smiled at the expectant faces around her. "Now, take a number and pair up with the person who has the same number as you. We will have seven minutes for the first person to be the dreamer, then we will reconvene for our shamanic drumming session to re-enter each other's dreams between dreamers."

Nuala found herself paired with an older woman, who could have been anywhere from a hard-lived late forties to early sixties. Johanna, whose puffy face, reddened eyes and solemn countenance indicated a troubled soul, had seemed to stay aloof from the rest of the group. Nuala had noticed her earlier. She had hesitated by the door as if debating whether to enter or not. Nuala wondered what sorrows were weighing her down. They found a quiet corner of the room to chat, and Nuala asked Johanna if she'd like to go first.

"I'm pretty new to all this," Johanna began. "I'm not even sure it's such a good idea for me to be here, but I guess I was desperate. If I can relate my dream first, I'll get the hang of how to respond to your dream."

Johanna bit her nail and Nuala noticed that all her fingernails were bitten down to the quick. When Johanna noticed Nuala's gaze, she clasped her hands in her lap and continued. "First, I have to say that I'm here to try to get in touch with my son, who died a few months ago. I've tried going to mediums and Seánces, but that didn't seem to work for me. I saw a video on the Interweb—I was searching on my son's computer to try to understand his state of mind when he died—that talked about this dreamwork group, and decided to give it a try. I have been plagued with some very unsettling dreams since his suicide."

Nuala reached out and touched Johanna's forearm in a gesture of sympathy. "I'm so sorry to hear of your loss. Please tell me your dream and we'll take it one step at a time."

~

The gong from a singing bowl indicated it was time to regroup. Once all were settled, Shelagh began to recite in her soothing voice, "Close your eyes, sit comfortably. We will begin our journey by acknowledging our energy centres.

Tune in to your body, your spine. Bring your awareness to your root chakra. You may see the colour red. Feel yourself sending down roots into the earth, gathering energy up into your body through the soles of your feet …"

Nuala opened one eye and glanced surreptitiously over at Johanna. The older woman was fidgety and picking at her cuticles again. Nuala was also having a hard time concentrating as she kept going over and over Johanna's story in her mind. That poor thing. She knew their partnership this evening was fortuitous; she wanted to offer some comfort to this grieving mother. She tried to tune back to Shelagh's guided meditation.

"Feel the energy flowing up through your body, moving up to your sacral chakra, your water element …"

I'm so thirsty. I forgot my water bottle in the car. Dang!

"Now gently bring your awareness up to your third chakra, your fire element, represented by golden yellow …"

Fire element. Nuala gave an involuntary shudder as she thought back to her escape from a fiery death. Was it over a year ago now? Seems like yesterday she thought she was going to die in a church, of all places. But that, too, was fortuitous, as it was the occasion of her introduction to Seán. It had taken some time for them to reconnect, but with him now recovering at the inn from his recent fall, things were progressing quite nicely. Good things can come from dark and horrible experiences. She wanted to help Johanna experience the same. *Focus ... focus ... breathe deep ...*

"... crown chakra, violet-white, the highest of the main chakras. Here there is a golden sun hovering over the top of your head, a portal through which you can connect to the Divine Source of all light and truth. You may also visualise this portal as a thousand-petalled lotus representing infinity and eternity. As you become aware of this unity with the Divine, whatever that is for you, you are now pulsing with cosmic energy; here you can re-enter the dream—yours or your partner's—and gain further enlightenment about its meaning."

Shelagh began a rhythmic beat on a waist-high drum—a deep, steady thrumming that provided the background to the participants' journey into their waking dreams ...

~

An hour later, Nuala was waiting outside the hall for Johanna to emerge. "What did you think of your first dreamwork session?"

"I enjoyed it. I'm surprised, as I didn't hold out much hope that it would help, but I got some comfort from the experience. Your suggestion that the house I was trapped in represents my body and the grief trapped inside makes sense. I'm going to go home and try out the mantra Shelagh mentioned for healing. What was it now ..." Johanna rummaged in her large, worn, shoulder bag until she came up with a torn piece of lined paper. "Ah, here it is. I had to write it down. My memory is not what it used to be ... 'I love you. I'm sorry. Please forgive me, and thank you.' I didn't even try to write down the original Hawai'ian she said at first." She folded the paper and tucked it back into her bag before continuing.

"I hope that will help me to forgive my son for leaving me so suddenly. But I still wish I could see him one more time ... to know he is well and happy now."

"Um, that's what I wanted to talk to you about." *It's now or never.* Nuala dove in. "My sister has a gift. She's often visited by departed loved ones. I could ask her to try to reach out to your son."

Johanna shook her head and said, "I don't know ... I've visited mediums before, and it didn't do any good. It gets my hopes up for nothing. Thank you for your kindness tonight, though."

"Moira isn't a medium, exactly. She doesn't advertise and most times she doesn't seek out the visitations. In fact, she probably won't be too happy that I even suggested this to you, but I couldn't leave tonight without mentioning it.

I can talk to her and then get back to you next month, if you plan to be here again?"

"Well, I suppose it can't hurt. Alright, I'll plan to be here. I'm going to try to do better about recording my dreams the first thing when I wake up so I can remember them. And then 'seeding' my dreams with a request for a specific kind of dream I can remember. You all have such vivid recollections of such interesting dreams. It's kind of fun, even if I don't get a personal visit from my son."

"Well, you know, next month's meeting is on November third. That's a couple days after Samhain when the veil is extra thin between worlds. It's a great time to ask for a visitation dream."

"Hmmm. I didn't know that. You are so knowledgeable about these things. Thank you for your help and coaching tonight. Do you live here in Ballydehob?"

"I'm down in Schull. This is the nearest dream group I could find. You?"

"I've got a little cottage between here and Schull." She brightened, "But Denny was buried in Schull. It's where our family is from. That, and the local priest in Ballydehob refused to perform the funeral Mass."

"Oh, I'm so sorry! That must have hurt awfully!"

"Well, he said he wasn't available and suggested I go to Schull, but I know it's because of the way Denny died.

I haven't been to Mass there since."

"Well, I'm glad we met, and I hope I can be of assistance in the future. Since you are on the way for me, can I give you a lift next month?"

"That would be grand."

They exchanged contact information and parted ways. Nuala was pleased to see a bit more of a bounce in Johanna's step as she walked away. Now she had to find the right way to bring up Johanna's situation to Moira.

Chapter Thirty-Eight

"May the road rise up to meet you. May the sun shine warm upon your face, and the rain fall soft upon your fields, and until we meet again, may God hold you in the palm of his hand."

—Old Irish blessing

"I call this meeting of Gallagher Investigations to order," Moira said, looking at her sisters gathered around the kitchen table at the inn. It was their monthly meeting to check in and discuss potential cases. "Deirdre, would you like to provide a recap of the month?"

"Things have been pretty quiet lately," Deirdre commented, "Just the case of the missing toddler our neighbour asked us to help with last week."

"Wait, what was that about? I didn't hear about that case." Nuala looked back and forth between Moira and Deirdre.

"It wasn't a big deal; we figured it out in a short time. Mrs. Delaney on our street called the gardaí and all the neighbours in to help her find her little Tommie. He'd been missing for over an hour. Moira and I found him curled up asleep in his bedroom closet."

"Nothing supernatural or nefarious about it," Moira added.

"Well, Mrs. Delaney was no less grateful for our help, regardless," Deirdre said. "She had been frantic when she couldn't find him. What about this rash of burglaries that have been in the news lately? Anyone have any connections through which we could get involved in that?"

"No, but I do have a situation I've come across that I thought could benefit from Moira's special gift …" Nuala looked down at her hands as she twisted her fingers. She was hoping Moira wouldn't be upset that she had already somewhat committed her assistance with Johanna.

"And what is that?" Moira's eyes narrowed at Nuala's coy tone.

"Well, I was at my dreamers' group a few nights ago and met this woman. Her name is Johanna," Nuala began. "Her son committed suicide a few months ago and she is making herself ill with worry for his eternal soul. I thought you might be able to get in touch with him to give her some peace, you know, reassurance that he is okay."

"Nuala, you know it doesn't work that way. I can't just summon someone from the Otherworld. *They* come to *me* when they choose, or, when they're allowed. I'm not sure which it is, but I do know I don't have much control over it," Moira said. "I don't feel comfortable taking on the responsibility of this woman's mental state at the death of her son."

"I know, I know. I just thought if you knew about it you could send out some vibes or something?" Nuala didn't know how it worked, but she did know that Moira had a connection with the dead. Surely this was a worthy cause that warranted her effort.

"I'm going to these dreaming sessions to try to be of help to you and Deirdre in your work. I thought if I could become more adept at lucid dreaming then I could get some insights to help with cases. And I *am* getting better. I've been keeping a dream journal, and writing down my dreams first thing in the morning has helped me to remember them more clearly. I thought if we all seeded our dreams to request a dream visitation from an ancestor or messenger concerning Johanna's son, one of us might make contact."

"Nuala, it should be this woman's—Johanna's? — prerogative to receive a dream visitation, not ours."

"Aye, but she's so new to dreamwork and is grieving

so. I couldn't help offering our ... *your* ... help."

"So, you've already committed us?" There was a note of excitement in Deirdre voice.

"Well, I said I'd get back to her at the next meeting. But she gave me her phone number so, if you want, I could ring her and try to get more information?"

"Okay, but be sure she understands that we make no promises." Moira's kind heart was something Nuala had been counting on.

"Great, thanks. I'll ring her this afternoon. That way you'll have the information before you and Deirdre head back to Dublin this evening."

"On another note, how are things going here at the inn?" Moira was great at keeping the meeting agenda moving along.

"We're booked through the end of the year, so, grand," Nuala responded.

"I think Moira was referring to your nursing duties," Deirdre chimed in.

Nuala blushed at the reference to Seán. "He's doing much better. One month down, two to go before the cast will come off his leg, but he's starting to get around on crutches. Ma is his devoted attendant—they are getting along just grand."

"I'll need to go up and chat with him after this about

some of the renovations at the estate. We were there last weekend to check on things and not much seems to be happening," Deirdre said.

"It's a challenge to get workmen to show up when they say they will. I'm so glad he decided not to sell, but it is frustrating when he's not able to be on-site. He appreciated our help in clearing up the little matter of its haunting though."

"That was quite the adventure, wasn't it?" Deirdre said.

"Definitely a life-changing adventure for Nuala. Well, if there's no other business, we'll adjourn until next month," Moira said, closing the meeting.

That afternoon as Deirdre and Moira were packing up the Mini Cooper, Nuala came running out waving a piece of paper.

"Denny was twenty-three when he died back in April. He was almost finished with uni and had a job offer that he was excited about, so Johanna can't understand what made him take his life. She found him hanging from the rafters in the barn when he was home during spring break. Didn't leave a note. He was her only child."

"Okay, thanks, Nuala. I'll let you know if anything or anyone comes through." By then Dymphna was on the doorstep to see them off as well, and with hugs and snacks for the road, they were on their way.

~

The tall, thin man left the AA meeting at the Cork City Grange Hall and slid into the van that was waiting for him at the kerb.

"Well, these meetings aren't nearly as fun as the ones down in Ballydehob with those dreamers, but I got some leads tonight. Couple people commiserating on how hard it's going to be on their upcoming holidays to stay away from the pints with everyone around having a gargle. Got some names for ya to look up and approximate times their places will be empty."

"Fair play. Yer finally earning your keep. What's yer next group?"

"Got the Cork Hikers next Thursday. They're deciding who's going to hike the Pulleen Loop the following weekend. That's a big one, as it will be two hours' drive to the trailhead at Beara Way, at least two hours to hike, then two hours back. Here's the thing—as much as I dislike all this outdoorsy stuff, I think I should go on the hike, so as to not raise suspicions. You'll have to get Mickey to pull this one with you."

"Aw, he's a useless scut! If work was the bed he'd sleep

on the floor. Rather be in the pubs than earning a living, but I see yer point. Okay, get me the list by Friday so we can plan the best places to hit."

Chapter Thirty-Nine

Beneath this stone lies Katherine my wife
In death my comfort, and my plague through life
Oh liberty! but soft I must not boast
She'll haunt me else, with her ghost.

—From a Belfast tombstone

"I'm headed to Donnybrook this afternoon, need anything while I'm out?" Moira called to Deirdre on her way out the door.

"Naw. Doing a bit of research on Nuala's suicide case?" Deirdre was always one step ahead, as if reading Moira's mind.

"I don't know if I'd call it research, but a cemetery is as good a place as any to invite a spirit to come through," Moira replied. "I haven't had any visits from Denny in dreams or waking, so I'm going to do a little prodding."

"Good luck."

"Thanks, I feel like I'm going to need it on this one."

Moira drove the five minutes to Donnybrook Cemetery. She pulled into the parking lot of the Donnybrook Garda Station next door to the cemetery, as she'd need to get the key to the cemetery gate from them. It was one of her favourite thinking spots in the city, so Garda McDermott at the front desk recognized her and handed over the log book for her to sign out the key.

"Be long, Miss?" she asked.

"I never know. I hope less than an hour, though," Moira offered.

"Here you go, then."

Moira unlocked the padlock on the iron gate, let herself in, then replaced the lock behind her. She liked the idea of being the only living person amongst the dead in this quiet little spot hidden away in the bustling city. She made her way to the centre of the cemetery and sat at the garden bench next to the only remaining wall of the original Celtic Church of Saint Broc dating back to the first century. The oaks and maples throughout the cemetery had begun to shed their leaves of red and gold. A slight breeze rustled them into a pile at her feet.

She soaked in the peace of the place and sent up a whispered petition to the Universe: "Spirit guides, ministering angels, departed souls, give me guidance now to help Johanna find peace. Denny, if you can, and desire to reach out, I am listening."

Then she waited.

And waited. *I wish I were as good at meditation as Deirdre is; that would probably help me to clear my mind and focus on opening a space for Denny to reach me. What was that mantra she taught me the other day? Lumen De Lumine ... Lumen De Lumine ... Lumen De Lumine ...*

Despite the unseasonably warm sunshine dappling the sarcophagi around her, she felt a sudden chill. He appeared on the path in front of her, head bowed in an attitude of shy hesitancy.

"Denny?"

"I've done a bad thing. I can't stay long. I'm so sorry. Will you tell her I'm sorry? I tried to tell her myself, but she can't hear me."

"Of course. Taking your own life is a troubling thing; it doesn't make you bad. Your state of mind, the circumstances, all is taken into account, I'm sure, and you are never out of the reach of God's love," she consoled. She knew these things to be true from her many interviews with the departed, and her heart ached for this young man.

"Oh, I know that—I've felt that Love, for sure. As soon as I arrived here it hit me in the chest and spread out to all my extremities. It's not that—the bad thing—it's not my dying. I didn't take my own life. I was murdered."

Wasn't expecting that ... but then, why shouldn't the Universe move in synchronicity to bring this wrong to my attention if I can make it right? After all, isn't that my calling? Why else would I have this gift of being able to interact with the dead if not to be of help?

"Tell me."

"I'm so ashamed. Ma was so proud of me; the first person in our family to go to uni. I was doing well, but it all became too much. I'd taken a night job at the vet clinic where I had a permanent position waiting after graduation. I was responsible for cleaning out the cages and mopping up the clinic after hours. It wasn't hard work, but it was cutting into my study time, and I'd find myself falling asleep as soon as I'd get home. My grades were tanking, so I got into a study group to try to bolster my exam scores.

"There were three of us, lads I didn't know very well, but I didn't have a lot of friends and they were willing to take me into their group. One of them brought his girlfriend so she made the fourth. We had a big exam coming up and I was struggling with the material; we all were. One afternoon, Susan arrived at our session and presented us with a copy of the exam questions. She'd nicked them from the professor's desk somehow.

"I didn't want to do it, but by association I was in it already, and I needed this grade. We took the exam and we all passed, of course, being careful to not get every question right. But it was eating at me. I was sick thinking of what I'd done. I was determined to confess and take my punishment, even though I knew that meant I probably wouldn't graduate. I told the lads and Susan at our last session what I was planning to do and they gave out stink. They threatened and reasoned and I backed down. I admit I was scared.

"Then we had spring break and I went home. I guess they thought I would confess to Ma or even the priest, and that would be the end for them as well. They must have followed me home. They caught me the next morning when I went out to milk the cows, give Da a break with the chores while I was home. The lads jumped me and dragged me up to the loft. It was over in a blink. I found myself here in the Otherworld and the decision to turn myself in taken from me."

"Who were they? Who did this to you?" Moira was on fire with indignation.

"I don't want to cause trouble. I just want Ma to not worry for my soul, thinking I was a suicide and all."

"But—"

"Please, tell her I'm sorry and I'm okay," his words were faint as his presence began to fade. Then he was gone.

Moira sat a while longer, trying to gather her thoughts

and composure. Visitations were always a bit unsettling, but this one, with the jarring information of Denny's murder, left her in a turmoil as to what she should do. She had only one name: Susan.

When Moira got home, she recounted her meeting with Denny to Deirdre. "This kind of message needs to be delivered in person. I've already called Nuala and she has arranged for me to meet with Johanna on Saturday. Do you want to go back down with me?"

"I think I can be of better use here. I was going to spend the weekend at Seán's place and check on what the workmen are doing. They were supposed to start on the roof this week. Depending on if Johanna wants to pursue this—and I can tell that *you* want to pursue this—while you're gone, I could check the school alumni records for the most recent graduating class. How many graduates named Susan can there be?" Deirdre reasoned.

"Um, a lot ... but I was thinking we could also check with the department chair at the College of Veterinary Medicine. Nuala says that's what Denny was studying. Don't you have some contacts over there?" Deirdre's wide circle of friends and acquaintances had come in handy several times in the past and she didn't disappoint now.

"My boss knows the dean. He golfs with him on Friday afternoons and we've chatted a few times while he was waiting. I'll see what we'd need to do to get that information. You're not thinking of going to the garda at this point?" she asked.

"I need to talk that over with Johanna first. And what exactly would I tell them? Denny's death was ruled a suicide. What evidence could I give for re-opening the case at this point?" Moira had been ridiculed and given the brush off too many times in the past to go into this without careful preparations first.

"Right. Sounds like a plan. Saturday, then. We'll compare notes when you get back."

Chapter Forty

"We are so captivated by and entangled in our subjective consciousness that we have forgotten the age-old fact that God speaks chiefly through dreams and vision."

—Carl Jung

"I had a strange dream last night," Nuala began as she and Moira sat on the porch behind the inn waiting for Johanna to arrive. "I was hoping you might have some insights."

It was a soft day, the mist not quite visible but still causing a dampness to settle everywhere. Moira wrapped her jumper tighter around her and raised her eyebrows.

Nuala began, "I dreamed there was some government disaster and I was put in charge; I was the Taoiseach of Ireland. You and Deirdre did the swearing in, but it was private—no one knew about it—so I had to keep explaining to everyone that I was in charge now. There was a bit of lucidity to it, as there was a radio on in the background and I kept trying to turn it down in order to hear people around me better, but the volume control wouldn't work right. In the dream I remember thinking: this is an indication that I'm in a dream, because I'm having trouble getting technology to work right."

"Your right, that is a good indicator. Hmm. What an interesting dream. If it were my dream, I'd think about what it means to me to be Taoiseach."

"It means to be in charge. To make decisions. To be in the know."

"And who in your life is like that?"

"Um ... you?"

Moira laughed. "You want to take my place? You want to be me?"

"Once again, you've opened my eyes. Aye, nay. I don't want to be you; I want to be a bigger part of what you do. I think it's interesting that in my dream you and Deirdre were the ones who did the swearing in. I seek your approval and acceptance."

"Well, that's nothing new; you've been doing that since you were a toddler following us around. Alright then. This is your case. You take the initiative with Johanna today and I'll follow your lead."

"Really? That's grand! What should I say?"

Before Moira could respond, Dymphna appeared at the garden door with Johanna. "Your guest has arrived."

"Thanks, Ma. Johanna, so good to see you. Come in. Or, I guess I should say, come out ..." Nuala's nervousness at being the lead came out in a quick giggle.

"Thanks for seeing me." She turned to Moira. "You must be Nuala's sister, Moira. Does this mean you've made contact with my Denny?"

"It's so nice to meet you. Nuala has told me a few things about your situation, and aye, Denny did visit. He seems like a fine young man." She had a habit of speaking of the dead in the present tense, which tended to unnerve some, but Johanna didn't bat an eye.

"Please tell me! How was he? What did he say?" Johanna had grabbed hold of Moira's hands so Moira led her to a chair and guided her into it before letting go and settling into her own seat.

"He is worried about you. He doesn't want you to be sad or grieving for him—he's in a good place."

"Did he tell you why he took his life?"

"Johanna, Denny told me he did *not* take his own life. He was murdered."

"Murdered! Jaysus, Mary, and Joseph!" Johanna crossed herself, "Did he say who did it?"

"Well, not exactly. He was having difficulty in his

classes and was talked into cheating on an exam. His remorse led him to decide to confess to his teacher and the administration. His fellow students took matters into their own hands to prevent that from happening, which would impact their own futures. He wouldn't give me their names."

"Oh, my poor, poor boy! My good lad! What is to be done?"

Here Nuala chimed in, "That depends on what you want to be done. Would you like to pursue this? Even though Denny said he didn't want to cause his classmates trouble? And what about your husband? What does he think of all this?"

"We can't let them get away with this. Denny always did have a big heart, but I need to see justice done. As to my husband, well, I might as well be a widow for all that. Christmas last year Denny gave his da an iPod and headphones. Since Denny's death, all William does is walk around with those bloomin' things on his ears, oblivious to me and the world around him."

"Johanna, you need to talk to him about this. I'll need a letter from the both of you authorising me to act on your behalf—on Denny's behalf—with the school. Also, if you can think of any names Denny may have mentioned. Perhaps if I," she looked at Nuala, "*we* could have a look in Denny's room? Do you still have any of his things?"

"Same as he left 'em."

"I need to get back to Dublin," Moira said, "but Nuala, will you go to Johanna's sometime in the next few days and look for anything that may help us? And send me Johanna's letter when it's ready."

"Sure thing," Nuala stood and embraced Johanna, kissing her on the cheek. "I know we haven't known each other long, but I feel we have a bond now. Thank you for trusting us with this; we'll do what we can to make it right."

Chapter Forty-One

*"The Universe puts things in your way. The
more you pay attention to the synchronicities,
the more they will appear."*

—Jessica Siemers

n Monday, the letter from Johanna and William Fitzpatrick appeared in Moira's inbox along with a note from Nuala:

Hope this is what you need. I'm going to go this afternoon and talk with Father Halligan at St. Mary's. He conducted the funeral for Denny back in April. Johanna remembers several young people at the service who said they were friends of Denny's, but she didn't recognize all of them. I thought that would be a good place to start in the event the study mates were cheeky enough to show up at the funeral. Also, no cell phone for Denny in his room. Johanna said he always had it

with him, but it wasn't on him in the barn when they found him. She's given me his computer—no password on it—Seán is going through that as well. Cheers, N.

"We could use a peek at those phone records. Too bad we don't have enough to go to the gardaí yet," Deirdre sighed.

"Tell me about your experience at the university. Did your connections get you in to see the dean?" Moira asked.

"Well, not the dean, but he sent me to the Registrar. He said the list of graduates is a matter of public record so he had no problem giving me that. What he wouldn't give me was Denny's transcripts so I could see what classes he'd taken and who his instructors were."

"Have you gone over the lists of graduates? Anyone named Susan?"

"There are three. Which is much better than I'd anticipated." Deirdre pulled the printout from her messenger bag and handed it to Moira.

"There are probably only a couple hundred students in the graduating class; we're lucky," Moira commented, glancing at the sheet.

"See here, I've highlighted the Susans. There's Susan Duggan, Susan Sinclair, and Susanna Tobin. I thought we could check the white pages for any matches. Do you have a strategy yet for approaching them?"

"I'm working on it. I thought maybe something like we are family friends making a Book of Remembrance for his mum and wanted tributes from his friends to include in the book."

"Ooh, that's good. Nothing official about that. We could talk to them as if we're assuming they are friends—like we already know about them from things Denny might have said. Put some fear into 'em!" Deirdre's enthusiasm was encouraging.

"You think so? Should we go together, or divide and conquer again?"

"We don't have any other leads at the moment, do we? We know from Denny that this Susan, whichever one it is, cheated on her exams. We don't know if she was part of the murder, but she is a 'person of interest.' We should go together. Strength in numbers, and all that," Deirdre suggested.

With many Duggans and Sinclairs, and only one Tobin, none of which specified the first name of Susan within the greater Dublin area, they decided to attack the project fresh in the morning. They were both free from eleven to three, and then Deirdre had a meeting at the law office. They opted for personal visits rather than phoning, to better gauge reactions to their queries. If they struck out with the preliminary list, they'd have to widen their search.

Deirdre had printed up a flyer to hand out as well. It displayed a photo of Denny that Nuala had sent and a brief request for tributes. They debated about including their phone number, which could be traced to their address, and finally opted to use Moira's old Hotmail address.

Almost two hours into their labours they'd gotten many blank stares and a few more with no one home. "I'm starving," Moira moaned. "Let's stop for a bite."

"No need to stop; I packed us a lunch. It's in the boot." Ever prepared, Deirdre came through once again. As they munched pasties, they reviewed their progress or lack thereof.

"Let's try the one Tobin. There's a Susanna listed as a relative to the head of house, and I know it's not the same name exactly, but at least we'll knock it off the list. The address isn't far from here." Deirdre had methodically coded the list with symbols indicating their various results and mapped a route that was most efficient.

As a precaution, they parked a few doors down from the neat, little cottage on a side street set in the outskirts of the city. An older woman with long grey hair hanging in a braid down her back answered the door. She was wearing a smock and wiping her hands on a dish rag.

"May I help you?" She asked politely.

Deirdre led, "Hello, we're friends of Denny

Fitzpatrick. We're looking for Susan."

"You must mean my daughter, Susanna," she turned and called into the room behind her, "Sue, darling, it's someone for you."

A twenty-something came to the door. Statuesque and perfectly groomed, her blonde tresses fell to past her shoulders in thick waves. She would be called beautiful by some, but for a sour expression on her face that was in opposition to her appearance.

"What is it?" She asked briskly.

"We're friends of Denny—" Moira was quick to observe a slight blanching behind the careful makeup, but it was quickly gone.

"Who? I don't know any Denny."

She turned away but her mum blurted, "Wasn't there a Denis that came here once with yer fella to study?"

"Ma, I'll handle this. Go back to what you were doing." Turning to the girls she said, "What is this about?"

"We're friends of Denny Fitzpatrick, who died last spring. We heard you were one of his friends from uni and thought you might like to participate in a tribute book we're gathering for his mum. You know, what you liked about him, something you may have done together?"

"Where did you hear we were friends? I barely knew him. He came once to a study session with … my friend, but

I wouldn't call him a friend; more of a friend of a friend."

"Okay, well can you tell us where we can find the friend who brought Denny to your study group? We want to be sure to include all Denny's friends in the tribute book."

"I don't feel comfortable giving out someone else's personal information. I'm sorry I can't help you more."

As the door began to close, Deirdre handed her the flyer. "Thanks for your time. Here—in case you think of something you'd like included in the tribute."

The woman took the flyer and stared after them as they walked away.

Back in the Mini, Moira was shaking, "That's her. It's got to be. All I could think of was, what a clannógach. It's perfect—someone with luxuriant, tressy hair, yes, but there's a double meaning of one who is sly or cunning. That cailin is hiding something."

They had waited a bit in the car after the encounter, as Moira was still somewhat shaken. It was fortuitous that they had, for moments later they saw a car pulling out of the drive, and the very cailin herself driving off at a fast clip.

Moira looked at Deirdre and they both grinned. Moira started up the car and they set off, at a discreet but manageable distance. They didn't drive long before Susanna's metallic red Honda Jazz pull into a drive.

"Note the address while I drive past," Moira

instructed. Looking back, Deirdre saw a young man open the door as Susanna rushed in, clutching their flyer.

"Two identified, one to go," Deirdre said. "Let's look up the address in reverse white pages when we get home. We should be able to get a name to go with that face."

Chapter Forty-Two

"And the graves were opened and many bodies of the saints which slept arose and came out of the graves...and appeared unto many."

—Matthew 27:52-53

Nuala wrapped her arms around herself as she walked the aisle of St. Mary's Church, looking for Father Halligan. His housekeeper said he was here, and to go on in, but she still got a creepy feeling in old churches after the incident in St. Brendan's in Cloghane. The closing of a door made her start, but then she saw the priest coming out of the Sacristy.

"Father Halligan, thanks for taking time to see me today."

"Of course, Nuala. I have a couple of new altar boys coming in for training in a bit; do you mind if we sit here in the nave?"

"That'll be grand. This won't take long." Nuala followed him into a pew and turned to face the kindly old man who had known her most of her life.

"What's this all about? Something about a funeral service a few months back?"

"For Denny Fitzpatrick. Do you remember?"

"I do—the suicide." A frown appeared on his face.

"That's the one, but I've, *we've*, my sisters and I have been talking with Johanna Fitzpatrick, Denny's mum. She's thinking of asking the gardaí to re-open the case as a suspected murder."

"Murder! Why would she think such a thing?" Father Halligan started up from the pew in agitation.

"Well, there were little signs, like his cell phone gone missing, and his making plans to meet with a friend the next day."

Father Halligan seemed speechless, so Nuala continued, "Anyway, I was wondering if you noticed anything or anyone suspicious at the funeral? Anyone there you didn't know?"

"Well, there were his parents, cousins, aunts, his friends from secondary school and up." he paused. "And it was nice to see a few friends from university make it down for him."

Nuala perked up. "Did you meet them? Talk with

any of those uni friends?"

"Well, there was one young man; he seemed to be with another couple of youth, a lad and young lady, but he was the only one I spoke to. They had stood in the back near the door and left after the service, but this lad lingered a bit. When I approached him, he said an odd thing. He said he was surprised that Denny would be allowed burial in the churchyard.

"I assured him that although that used to be the case—and I remember not that long ago offering the Lord's Prayer for one such unfortunate in a nearby cillin—the church has broadened its perspective over the past decade. We make allowances for a disturbed state of mind that may have affected someone's actions. It's not our place to judge someone who takes his own life. We leave that up to God and are now allowed to give the departed a Christian burial in hallowed ground. He seemed relieved at my words, thanked me, and left."

"Did you not get his name, Father?"

"I did not; I'm sorry, my dear. But wait! He may have stopped at the guest registry by the door before he went out. I can check it if you'd like. The Fitzpatricks left without taking it home with them that day and I've not had an opportunity to bring it to them. If I gave it to you, would you take it to them for me? Unless ... you did say 'murder' earlier? Maybe I should be handing it over to the gardaí ..."

"It's not an official investigation at this point, Father. It's my sisters and I having our suspicions. But I would appreciate a look and for sure pass it to Johanna for you."

"Your sisters! Is Moira still after talking with her little friend, Julia, who died these many years ago now? I don't know as I should be encouraging these fantasies of hers. Is that what this is about?"

"Not at all, Father. It's Johanna who asked us to check out a few things—you know, the cell phone and all. We just want to help."

She walked with him to the rectory next door where he retrieved the guest book.

"Here you go. Give my regards to your mum. I know she usually attends early morning Mass what with the running of the inn and all, and I try to delegate that one to my assistant curate. As a result, I haven't seen her in a bit. Is she doing alright?"

"Sure, and she's grand, Father. Thanks again for seeing me. I appreciate it." And with that, Nuala left the old gent to get on with his priestly duties.

Chapter Forty-Three

During Samhain our ancestors too, are more available to us—especially in our dreams.

—Old Irish Folk Tradition

Monday Evening, November 2, 2010, Ballydehob

The room was buzzing with voices as the group of about fifteen people waited for Silverbird Moonbeam to get the meeting started.

"... went to the cemetery on Samhain to get a better vibe for my dreams ..."

"I got nothing. Well, nothing I remember, anyway. I'm no good at this."

"... really creepy stuff. I screamed and woke myself up."

"... not sure I'd even come tonight ..."

"... in a state last night so not my best today ..."

From the back of the room, Nuala noticed a tall, thin

man, late thirties, who seemed to wander from group to group, only engaging in a few pleasantries here and there. She'd seen him here before. Difficult not to notice the hard features and straight dark hair pulled back into a low ponytail, but something about him this evening gave off a creepy vibe. He caught her eye and she nodded but looked quickly away, addressing Johanna next to her.

"Anything exciting come to you on Samhain?" Nuala inquired.

"Well, not my Denny, but I saw a great black wall that seemed to go on forever. I was walking past it, looking for a way through. For some reason I *needed* to get through, when suddenly there were dots of light breaking through the blackness in several spots. The further I walked, the more lights I saw, until the wall crumbled away in a blaze of light. I couldn't even look at it for hurting my eyes. What do you think it means?"

"We can go through the dream interview together afterwards if we don't get partnered together this time. I think there's some great meaning there, though."

Johanna smiled but she was looking past Nuala. Nuala turned in time to see the tall man coming towards them. He extended his hand and said, "How ya doin', hey? I'm Brent. I've seen you here before."

"Nuala. What's the craic? This is my friend, Johanna."

He nodded to Johanna, then turned again to Nuala.

"You're a decent one, fancy a pint after this?" He was close enough now that Nuala could tell he'd already downed a few before he'd arrived.

"I will, yeah?"

"She has a boyfriend," Johanna cut in.

Nuala gave her a dark look and was relieved when Shelagh/Silverstar sounded the gong, signalling all to gather. As the two moved away from Brent, Johanna began, "Sorry, sorry. I thought I'd help. I could see you were not wanting his company."

"I appreciate it, but the less a guy like that know of my business, the better I like it," Nuala said.

Nuala's dream partner was Fiona, the young girl about sixteen who had been coming each month with an older cousin.

"Go ahead," Nuala urged, "tell me your dream."

"Right. It's just a snippet of a dream, though. I'm taking frozen turkeys out of my freezer and putting them in my car to take to neighbours so they aren't all in my house. So many turkeys! I think they must be worth a lot of money and I'm afraid someone will break in to steal them so I'm giving them away. There are thieves who have my house bugged so they know what is in there." Fiona stopped and looked expectantly at Nuala.

"Okay, what would you title this dream?"

"Well, 'Frozen Turkeys,' I guess."

"And how did you feel when you woke up?"

"Worried that someone was going to break into my house! I know it's batty, and they were only turkeys, but it left me with a feeling of unease that I'm not safe."

"Could it be symbolic?" Nuala pulled out her battered copy of the Dream Codex. "It says here that a turkey symbolises a hidden emotion. Is there something you are feeling and not expressing?"

"Just ... worry about being robbed ..."

"Hmmm. Okay. What dream action do you want to take?"

"I'm going to ask my da to put better locks on the doors and windows."

"Does that mean you are thinking it could be a premonition?"

"Well, there have been lots of break-ins around this area lately, haven't you heard?"

"If this were my dream, I would think it could be a reflection of the times; a manifestation of fears from watching the telly. But I might also do as you suggest and be sure my house is secure."

Shelagh approached Nuala during the social gathering after the meeting. "How's your friend doing, what had the accident?"

"He's grand, thanks for asking," Nuala replied. "He'll be staying with Ma and me at the inn for another month or so, until he's better able to fend for himself, but he's starting to get around quite well on crutches."

"Didn't you say he inherited that big estate that was in the papers last year, up in Kildare?"

"Yes, but it will be some time before he'll be able to be on his own there."

"He's sure a lucky bloke to have you and your ma to take care of him."

"We're happy to have him," Nuala said.

Johanna joined them and suggested they start for home, if Nuala was ready.

"I am. See you next month, Shelagh. Thanks for a lovely session."

None of them noticed that Brent was lingering at the snack table within earshot of their conversation a bit longer than necessary to get a glass of lemonade and a piece of barmbrack.

~

Though it was close to eleven when Nuala finally arrived home, she tiptoed up to Seán's room and tapped softly on the door.

"Come in."

Nuala entered and found Seán on the computer searching family history websites. Since he'd been at the inn, Ma had gotten him hooked on genealogy. He was seeking information about his biological family—the grandparents and beyond whom he'd never known.

"Ah, glad you're back safely. Look here—my great-grandfather's brother was named Seán. Do you think that's whom I was named after?"

"Could be."

"How was your evening? Did Johanna enjoy the group? Has she had any dreams of her son?" Seán closed down the computer and swivelled his chair to face Nuala.

"No, not yet, but I think she is feeling more hopeful. Um, Seán … could I share something with you?"

"Of course. Here, sit on the bed. What is it?"

"I had a dream on Samhain Eve. It was too dear to discuss in the dream group this evening, but it has continued to weigh on me," Nuala began.

"I could tell something was bothering you," Seán encouraged.

"Well, you know we are looking into this business with Denny's murder. I don't see how you are involved in that at all, besides helping me with his computer, but …"

Seán waited patiently while Nuala gathered her thoughts.

"Alright. I had a dream. I was hoping for a visit from *someone*, seeing as how it was Samhain and all, and I had been doing so well to pay attention to my dreams for some time now. You know, honouring them. Well. It was Da. I'd only ever heard his voice before—remember when I was trapped in the church fire?"

"How can I forget? That's the day we met."

"Aye, so I was asking for some guidance, you know, if we should even get involved in this business. I mean, these people are murderers! Anyway, in the dream I was walking through a field and I saw Da coming towards me. I could tell it was him right off, his way of walking slow with a bit of swagger. He was dressed in white and stopped in front of me. I wanted to hug him but he put up his hand to stop me. He said, 'Listen!' So, I listened.

"He seemed to know a lot about you. He said it was a good thing you were on crutches; they'll come in handy. He also said you'd better dress warm—'bundle up,' were his words. I said, 'Da, what do you mean? I don't understand.' He smiled and said, 'Seány is a good 'un for ye. We're gonna protect him.'

"He then directed me to 'Look!' and I looked at this large stone I hadn't noticed before in the field. On it were some writings, and pictures. I saw a knife dripping with blood. Then a mist rose up and the stone and Da were gone."

"Ah, Nuala, it was only a dream—"

The look he got made him choke back his words. "I know you are worried about this case, but I'm not involved. I'm grand. No need to worry. I'm glad your Da approves of me though."

Nuala smiled at this nod to the validity of her nocturnal encounter. "Well, it's getting late. You need sleep to help you heal. I'll see you in the morning." She kissed him lightly on his lips, then she slipped out the door.

~

A few days later, no one was around to hear the sound of tinkling glass as the tall, slim figure deftly reached his arm through the broken window and opened the back door to the big house. He moved confidently—having previously disabled the ancient alarm system—to the front door and opened it to his partner who was waiting outside by the van. They usually pulled these jobs in daylight, moving as if they belonged, and it had worked well for them in the past. Here, with the house so remotely located and the owner away down in Schull romancing his cailín, they could work at their leisure.

They'd been in the business long enough to have developed an eye for what would sell, and made quick work of loading an assortment of armoires, side tables, lamps and bric-a-brac into the van. It sounded like it could be another month before the owner came home and by then they would be long gone.

Chapter Forty-Four

*Xiiair bhionn do láiiih i nibéal an mhadra,
tarraing go réig í.*

'When your hand is in the dog's mouth withdraw it gently.'

—Irish Proverb

The next morning Nuala called Moira and Deirdre to review the case and put together a plan going forward. They were all on speaker so even Seán could be a part of the conversation. They went over all that they knew so far. Moira reported that Ryan O'Toole was the name of the person Susan visited after their 'tribute book' fishing expedition.

"Have you been able to get anything off Denny's computer?" Moira asked.

Seán responded, "We found his study notes and a paper he was working on. Seems like the group was working on it together. It was divided into sectional assignments.

There were parts assigned to DF, JT, RO and MH. No emails that were suspicious."

Nuala filled her sisters in on her visit with Father Halligan. "The guest book from the funeral has a cryptic entry for one Martin, no last name, who wrote: 'sorry, mate.' That may be our third member of the group," she said.

"Hold on, hold on ... give me a minute ..." Deirdre said as she pulled out the list of grads from a folder and scanned it quickly. She had it mostly memorised anyway, and soon found what she was looking for—Martin Harkness. "Ha! The only 'Martin' and his last name starts with an 'H,' it's gotta be him!" She exclaimed with glee.

"That's grand, Deirdre; I think we've got three solid names now," Moira returned.

"What about the email you got yesterday? The one in response to our flyer? That's got to be from Ryan or Susanna," Deirdre interjected.

Moira pulled up the email, and read: *Would like to contribute to the remembrance book. Have some items I need to deliver in person or via Anpost. Please reply with a postal address. Cheers, Roger*

"What do you make of it," Deirdre asked.

"I think he's trying to locate us so he can, oh, I don't know ... murder us as well?" Nuala said.

"Do we go to the gardaí now, or set our own trap?"

Deirdre asked.

"How about both?" Moira suggested.

The plan was to respond to the email with their flat address, then wait, having the gardaí on speed dial. Seán was not happy with the plan. "I'm going to be there. You are not doing this on your own. That's taking a big chance." Seán was adamant.

"That means *I'm* going to be there as well, seeing as you aren't able to drive yet," Nuala said.

"I don't know how much help you can be, with your gimpy leg, and arm in a sling," Moira said. "But I agree it's better to have reinforcements. If you think you are up to the trip, you're welcome to come, but it could take a while. Or nothing could happen at all."

"Or something could happen," Seán countered grimly.

Once again Nuala enlisted the help of Molly Ronan to take over the inn kitchen for a few days. Molly couldn't begin until the weekend, so Nuala and Seán drove to Dublin on Saturday morning. Moira sent the email response with their address to 'Roger' as soon as Nuala and Seán arrived. They didn't anticipate that anything would happen before nightfall, so they supplied themselves with snacks and tucked in to wait.

Nuala shared Moira's room, and Seán camped out on the couch. They took shifts through the night but no one got much sleep. Three nights went by with no event to warrant the high vigilance, and even Moira was beginning to think it was a dead end.

"How long should we keep it up?" Deirdre asked.

"Let's give it a couple more days. If nothing happens by Thursday, I need to get back to Schull for the weekend. Molly was only available until then," Nuala said.

Tuesday evening, or more accurately, Wednesday morning at 3:00 a.m., Deirdre heard a noise. Being on the ground floor had its merits for access to the back garden, but it meant their flat was more accessible to an intruder. A pinpoint of light shown over the wall surrounding the garden. She didn't wait for confirmation, but immediately rang the local gardaí.

"Someone is breaking into our house! Please come right away!"

She gave the address, then tiptoed into the front room and nudged Seán. By then, Moira and Nuala were also awake and joining them. Deirdre had her keys laced between the fingers of one hand, and her Maglite flashlight in the other. Moira held her da's brolly and Nuala was armed with a can of spray deodorant. The sisters huddled behind the couch and Seán feigned sleep with his crutch at the ready, tight in his hands.

Even though they knew what was coming, it was still

a shock to hear the breaking of glass as the sliding door shattered. Frozen in place, they listened as someone kicked away the remaining shards and entered the room. A black-clad figure entered and headed towards the bedrooms. Seán lunged with his crutch as the figure passed the couch. The intruder stumbled, but quickly regaining footing, whipped around and slashed at Seán with a pocket knife.

Moira saw the lights of the gardaí vehicle and ran to the front door, flinging it open before the vehicle had stopped. Deirdre flashed the Maglite into the intruder's face, who then fell backward, tripping over a potted Ficus tree and collapsing among its now broken branches.

"Aye, fella, yer looking at five years just for having that knife on ya, whatever else is going on here," Garda Malone said as he yanked up the intruder and pulled off the balaclava.

There was a moment of stunned silence as the golden tresses of Susanna Tobin cascaded down.

"You're a lass," Garda Malone said, stating the obvious. He relieved her of the knife she still clutched in one hand. Addressing the other garda he said, "Keating, take statements while I get this one secured in the vehicle."

Garda Elinor Keating motioned Moira and Deirdre over to the couch where Nuala was already helping Seán off with his heavy winter coat and assessing any damage from Susanna's knife. Garda Keating sat across from them and asked, "Who wants to start?"

"I was awake and saw someone climb over the back wall," Deirdre began. "I'm the one who rang the station."

Garda Keating took in the Maglite, spray, and umbrella and said, "Expecting trouble, were ya? And you all bundled up for a hunting trip. Heating system failure?"

Now that the light was on, and the adrenaline rush was beginning to dissipate, Seán took stock of himself. There were several gashes in his jacket, but they hadn't penetrated to his skin. "I'm just visiting. Got a bit cold in the night and slipped on my jacket—"

"Look, Garda Keating, I'm going to be straight here," Moira interrupted. "We *were* expecting trouble. We came into some information that a friend's supposed suicide was actually a murder, and we seemed to have made the guilty parties nervous."

"'Came into some information' huh?" Garda Keating gave her a stern look, "Go on."

"This may take a while. Could we come into the station in the morning?"

"Very well, I'll need your names and addresses for now. Come to the station around ten and ask for me."

When they were alone, Deirdre turned to Moira and asked, "How much are you going to share?"

"All of it. I can't be hiding what I do. I would like to be of service and I can't do that if I can't be honest with the gardaí."

Seán had been unusually quiet and Moira now turned to him, "What's on your mind, Seán? How much of this do you think we should tell?"

"This is all so strange. Nuala, did you tell your sisters about your dream? Seeing your da?"

"I did not. You tell them."

Seán recounted what Nuala had told him, then added, "What I didn't say to Nuala as we were packing to come up here is that I kept having this nagging feeling to bring a heavy coat, even though the weather was supposed to be mild. I didn't have any of my own at the inn, so I checked with Dymphna and she gave me one of her husband's old hunting jackets. Last night, it wasn't that I was cold, but Da's message to "bundle up" kept rolling through my head until I finally got up and put the thing on. I think that saved me getting some nasty cuts just now." He showed them the tears in the jacket.

"For sure the Old Ones were looking after ya," Moira affirmed. "There's no such thing as a coincidence, Seán. It's called 'synchronicity;' it's those little nudges from beyond. You'll be seeing more of that the more you hang around the Gallagher girls!"

Chapter Forty-Five

> *"Being human is definitely cumbersome, but being a soul isn't. There will never be a moment when we can say we have arrived and the journey is over. Even when these bodies retire, we will still be in motion because we are made up of energy and energy is always in motion."*
>
> —Amanda Lux
>
> 'A Lone Traveler's Guide to the Divine' podcast

A mere six hours later, the foursome trouped into the garda station. Garda Keating ushered them into an interview room.

"Protocol is to interview you one at a time, but seeing as you are the obvious victims here, I think we can make short work of this." Nodding to Moira, she said, "Let's start with you."

Moira began, "What I am about to tell you may seem unbelievable, but you must know it is all the truth." She began back at the beginning, where she first was introduced to the Otherworld by visitations from her childhood friend. Garda Keating, to her credit, did not interrupt once, but sat there, expressionless, and listened.

"We felt we had to come up with some concrete evidence before we could go to the gardaí with our suspicions. Now, after the break-in which followed the email, which came from the flyer we delivered to Susanna, that should be proof enough to reopen the case of Denny's death."

"Miss Tobin has confessed to breaking in, but she says she was looking for cash and wasn't trying to hurt anyone. She was startled by Mr Kennedy's attack on her, and she was reacting in self-defence."

"That's pure rubbish!" cut in Seán.

"About the same amount of rubbish as you all just happened to have a Maglite, umbrella, and a spray can available at the instant Miss Tobin made her appearance? And you," here Garda Keating looked directly at Seán, "were dressed for a hunting expedition in the middle of the night in a heated apartment?"

"Sure look, in the spirit of telling all, I'll admit that I had some help there." Seán proceeded to tell of Nuala's dream and his prompting to bring a heavy jacket.

"You must think we are right langers, or away with the

fairies!" Moira cried. "If I hadn't experienced these things myself, I would have a hard time believing me."

"You're absolutely correct—your story would be unbelievable to someone who hasn't had experience with the Other Crowd." Garda Keating now had a slow smile start in the corner of her mouth. Moira, Deirdre, Nuala, and Seán all looked up from their fidgeting and sat up a bit straighter in their seats. "It seems you *are* being watched over in this adventure of yours, for of all the gardaí who could have responded to your call last night, and to take up your case today, you got me. I was filling in for a mate who got sick—I wasn't supposed to be there, but I was. I was named Elinor for my Gran, who often spoke with the Old Ones. She knew of things she couldn't have known any other way. Be assured, I do believe you. Now, if you will hand over the evidence for this crime that you have been so good as to gather for us, I think we can take it from here. We'll be getting in touch with—" she glanced through the notes at the top of the folder Deirdre passed to her— "Mrs. Fitzpatrick of Ballydehob." Garda Keating stood in dismissal.

Outside the garda station, Moira nearly collapsed as she stumbled down the steps. "What just happened?"

"I think we've been dismissed from the case," Deirdre replied.

"Well, this has sure been exciting. Now, do you want help with fixing that back door?" Seán asked.

"We can handle it. I'll ring the flat manager. Being a renter is much easier than being an estate owner. But thanks for all your help, Seán. For the moral support by just being here and then taking the worst of it from Susanna," Deirdre said.

"'Self-defence' my eye! She won't get away with that, will she?" Nuala was still fired up.

"We'll just have to wait and see, I guess." Moira sighed.

"While I'm up here, I thought I'd head over to Kildare and see what's happening at the estate. I can set up a few appointments while I'm at it. I've been talking with a security systems company about installing some state-of-the-art equipment. There's a couple camera's there now, but they are so antiquated a wean could bypass them. You could use an alarm system at your flat as well. I don't think you'll need something that high-tech, but at least some kind of warning if the windows or doors are tampered with," Seán said.

"Our landlord isn't going to go for that kind of expense. You can forget it," Deirdre complained.

"Let me look into it. I'm paying enough for the system at my place; they should throw in a few extras I could install here." Seán turned to Nuala. "You willing to drive me over to Kildare?"

"Of course!"

Once Seán and Nuala left, Deirdre approached Moira with her own idea for heightened security. "Let's get a dog!" Moira's sceptical expression caused Deirdre to hastily add, "Come with me to the SPCA and we can at least take a look."

"I don't know. We haven't had a dog since Reggie died ten years ago now. Pets are a lot of work."

"I'd certainly feel safer with a dog around. It can't be more expensive than a 'state of the art' security system," she reasoned.

"Well, I guess it wouldn't hurt to go look."

"Right; I've got the car keys, let's go. No time like the present!"

~

"Nothing too small. We want a dog that will intimidate an intruder." Walking the aisles of the cages, Moira's heart went out to each one of the forlorn and needy creatures she saw. If Deirdre had her way, they'd move to the country and adopt them all. They stopped at one beauty—a larger shepherd-sized dog who quietly gazed at them with penetrating hazel-gold eyes.

"What kind of dog is that?" Moira inquired of the staffer who was escorting them. "I've never seen a tail quite like that on any dog before."

"That's Suki, she's an Anatolian Shepherd—the breed are diggers and herders. She was left in a backyard with a bucket of dog food and a kids' wading pool full of water when the owners moved. Neighbours heard her barking and whining for days before investigating and calling Animal Control. She'd dug a big hole trying to get out of the yard, but hadn't quite made it before Animal Control got to her.

"She arrived here about a month ago, malnourished and covered in fleas and sores. She had to have surgery to remove a cyst on her neck, but she's mending nicely and is ready for her new forever home."

"What is wrong with people?!" Deirdre fists were clenched and she was trying hard to maintain control. "I hope the owners were fined or jailed or both. How can they sleep at night with that kind of behaviour on their conscience?"

"I don't know what the outcome was other than we got Suki, here," the staffer said. "But you are right, I would hope they aren't allowed to have any more animals."

"Can we interact with her?" Deirdre wanted to know.

"You can; let me get her leash."

Forty-five minutes later they had paid the deposit and set up an appointment for someone to come by and check out their flat. "Do you think it's too late to ask the landlord to get a back door that has a doggie flap in it?" Moira asked.

"Give him a ring," Deirdre encouraged, as she gave Suki a last kiss on her nose before they left.

Back in the Mini, Moira phoned the flat manager. They would have to amend their rental agreement and pay an additional pet deposit for any potential damages. He promised he'd check on the status of the door he'd ordered to swap it for one with a pet entrance.

"I think the landlord is feeling pretty bad about the break-in. He's very proud of the 'safe neighbourhood' promotions he puts out about the complex," Moira guessed.

"That's grand. More to our advantage. Let's get the messages on the way home. We need dog food, a bed for Suki, some chew toys…" Deirdre made some notes in her mobile listing the items.

"You're sure about this? The inspection is tomorrow, maybe we should wait 'til then," Moira suggested.

"Sure, we will. No big deal."

Moira's mobile trilled. As she was driving, she passed it to Deirdre. It was Nuala.

"Greetings, Sis, what's up?"

"We got to the house in Kildare and found someone had broken in. They came in through the back door, broken glass everywhere. Seán was right about the old security system being worthless." Nuala sounded breathless, like she'd been running from the burglars herself.

"Oh, no! Have the gardaí come? What's missing?" Deirdre had put her on speaker.

"They're on the way. Whoever did this had to know no one was around because it must have taken ages to empty several rooms of most of the furniture."

"Seán was saying there were a couple cameras still there. Has he checked to see if anything shows up? Strange that we'd have a break-in as well at the same time. I can't imagine the two are related, though," Moira mused.

"Seán and I are going to stay here at least overnight. The guys with the new security system can't get here until tomorrow. Seán had to pay extra to get them to come even that quickly. We'll head back to Schull after they finish up. I'll ring back when we know more. Luv ya, cheers."

Chapter Forty-Six

"We enter the world as strangers who all at once become heirs to a harvest of memory, spirit, and dream that has long preceded us and will now enfold, nourish, and sustain us."

—John O'Donohue, Excerpt from 'Benedictus.'

The next morning, Deirdre's first comment over breakfast was, "I had a dream."

"Sure, and tell me." Deirdre didn't often share her dreams, which made it special when she did.

"I saw Reggie. He was young and healthy again and he nudged my hand, like he used to do when he wanted to be let outside, or to be petted. I followed him and he led me to a box. I opened the box and Suki was in there, all huddled in a corner. I let her out and she and Reggie did that 'Down Dog' thing and started playing together. Do you think that means Reggie is my Spirit Animal? Do you think he wants us to adopt Suki?"

"If that really was your dream, and if it were *my* dream, I would definitely take it as a sign that we should adopt Suki."

"That's how I felt. And what do you mean, 'if that really was my dream'? You think I'm making it up to sway you?" Hands on hips, Deirdre looked at Moira, daring her to doubt.

"If it means that much to you, it's grand with me," Moira said softly.

They were interrupted by the ringing of Moira's mobile.

"Moira, Johanna Fitzpatrick here. I heard from a Garda Keating. I'm to go to the local garda station and give them a new statement concerning the things we've—you've—learned about Denny's death. Does this mean they think it's a murder case?"

"We hope so. We've given them all we've found. Would you like one of us to go with you? Nuala won't be back down your way until Friday," Moira said.

"I don't think so; I should be fine. Maybe I can get my husband to go as well …"

"You'll do grand. Give us a ring afterwards and let us know how it went."

Moira turned to Deirdre who had begun tidying up

in anticipation of the SPCA representative's visit. "Well, Garda Keating was as good as her word. They must still have Susanna in custody. I wonder if they'll pick up the other two?"

"I sure will feel better when Suki is here. How soon after the inspection did they say we can pick her up?"

"I believe it is any time afterwards. We can stop for the supplies on our way over there to get her."

"That will be grand. I'm so excited; I know she will be as good for us as we will be good for her."

~

While they waited for the security system installers to arrive, Seán and Nuala reviewed the camera images. They were grainy and at less-than-ideal angles, but they could see the large moving van parked in front with someone at the wheel. The backdoor footage showed a second person from the top of his head, with a bit of his forehead and nose in view.

"I'm not sure, but that kinda looks like a guy from the dream group. The long hair in a ponytail is pretty distinctive," Nuala said.

"What can you tell me about him?"

"His name is Brent. He's a bit creepy. He asked me to go for a pint after the session but I didn't encourage him. Should we show this to the gardaí?"

"I think we need to make a plan first."

"Do you have something in mind?"

"I have an idea, but we'd need to get your dream leader involved."

"Shelagh?"

"I guess. I've never met her. But if you say he's from the dream group, that may be where he learned my house was uninhabited. Do you remember mentioning anything about me when you were there?"

Nuala blushed at having Seán learn she had been talking about him. "Now that you mention it, Shelagh did ask about you, and I might have said something about you being down here with me and Ma until you were able to live in Kildare on your own."

"Could this guy have overheard you?"

"He's definitely the lurker type. He roamed around the room listening in on everyone, it seemed. He could have been listening to us. What do you want Shelagh to do?"

"Does she have some way to get in touch with the regulars, a post on her website or an email to people with notice of changes in the schedule for instance?"

"She does. Every session we sign in with our email address."

"Perfect. We set up a sting. She sends out a message

that something has come up and she'll be out of town on the day of the next meeting so she has to cancel. Then we wait at her place for him and his mate to show up with their truck."

"I don't know. Sounds dangerous. What would we do if he does show up?"

"Well, not us, exactly, acushla. We'll need to turn it over to the gardaí and have them be waiting. I don't want to put you or Shelagh in any danger."

Nuala was stunned for a moment at hearing the term of endearment from Seán. She quickly regained composure and said, "Right. The next meeting is December seventh. That means we have three weeks to get Shelagh on board and talk to whomever is investigating these break-ins. Shelagh lives in Ballydehob so I guess that means we contact the Ballydehob Garda Station."

"I'll do that, I'll show them these images. I've also got copies for the gardaí in Kildare. They can coordinate with their mates down there. I'd like you to talk to Shelagh though, give her a heads up and see if she's okay with all this."

~

To: *Ballydehob Dream group*

Cc Bcc

Subject: Class Cancelled

Greetings fellow dreamers!

I'm so sorry to have to do this, but I need to cancel class on Monday, December seventh. I've had a family emergency come up and I'll be out of town all day Monday. I'll be back Tuesday night. If anyone has any particularly juicy dreams they want to discuss, feel free to email me.

See you in the New Year!

Blessings and moonbeams,

Shelagh Silverstar

Chapter Forty-Seven

Fearr sean-fhiacha ná sean-fhala.
'Better old debts than old grudges.'
—Irish Proverb attributed to Flann Fina Mac Ossu

"I'm taking Monday off and going down to be with Nuala and Seán during this burglary business," Moira determined. "If you can afford the time as well, we could be there Saturday night and stay through Monday."

"I was thinking the same thing; it's a bit worrisome. I know the gardaí are handling it, but I'm worried that Nuala is going to want to be in the thick of it as well. Our first road trip with Suki! Can't wait for Ma to meet her. She mourned Reggie's passing almost as much as she did Da's."

Saturday evening arrived, and Suki was duly admired and petted by Ma, Nuala and various inn guests alike. Ma had gone out and bought a new ball and thrower to entertain Suki. She chucked the ball out into the back lawn, and everyone watched, including Suki, as it rolled to a stop about five yards away.

"Fetch, Suki!" Ma coaxed, "Go get the ball!"

Suki looked up at her with large, expressive eyes, as if to say, "You first."

Deirdre laughed. "Fetching balls is not her thing, Ma. She's more of a herder. Now if you run around, like this—" Deirdre started off at a sprint in the direction of the forlorn ball, and Suki took off like a shot right after her, nipping at her heels and running in circles around her. Deirdre collapsed in a heap of laughter and dog nuzzles. "Now, that's more her sport," she got out once she caught her breath and extricated herself from Suki.

Sunday evening the tone turned sombre as they began preparations to catch a thief. They had met with the gardaí and were given strict instructions to remain concealed inside Shelagh's neighbour's home, where Shelagh would be spending the night. Four gardaí would be located inside Shelagh's home awaiting the would-be thief. It was important to apprehend him in the actual act of breaking and entering and not before. From the images taken from Seán's surveillance camera, they knew the thieves had no problem working in daylight, so they were ready to go by six that morning and were hunkering down for a possibly long vigil.

By ten o'clock, Beatrice Buchanan, Shelagh's neighbour, set out tea and sandwiches for the group gathered at her home: Shelagh, Nuala, Moira, Deirdre, Seán, and Suki. Deirdre took Suki everywhere she could, wanting to help her feel safe with her new owners and overcome her abandonment issues. Deirdre was definitely Suki's person.

Seán, who had been sitting by the back door to the patio all morning with eyes glued to Shelagh's house, suddenly called out, "There's a white van pulling into the drive!"

Everyone jumped up and gathered around him. "Quiet! Quiet! Don't draw attention this way," he cautioned.

The trees between houses made it difficult to see what exactly was happening and the tension was palpable. About fifteen minutes passed, with no movement next door. Then the front door opened and two gardaí emerged with a man handcuffed between them. At that moment, the van door burst open and a second man took off at a dead run towards the back of the house. Nuala opened the patio door a crack to better hear what was happening. In a split second, Suki was out that door and in pursuit.

"Suki, no! Come back here!" Deirdre yelled, but her cries went unheeded as Suki had tunnel vision for her prey that was in need of herding.

The two remaining gardaí were also in pursuit, not

far behind Suki, but she had the speed, and soon overtook the man on the run. By now the group of watchers were out of range to see anything but they heard a distinctive yelp of a dog in pain. Deirdre and Moira both took off running at the sound. When they reached the group of now three men, one was on the ground being cuffed by a garda, and the third was bending over Suki lying on the grass.

"Suki! Oh, no!" Deirdre fell to her knees next to the dog. Suki wasn't moving and blood was coming from her mouth.

Chapter Forty-Eight

Is minic a bhris béal duine a shrón.
'It is often that a person's mouth broke his nose.'
—Irish Proverb

At the sound of Deirdre's voice, Suki opened her eyes, but didn't try to stand.

"I saw the bloke stop and give her a swift kick to the head. Caught her right on the side there, knocked her out for a bit, I imagine," Garda McClellan stated.

Using her jumper to gently wipe the blood from Suki's mouth, Deirdre said, "She's lost a couple teeth. That's where the bleeding is coming from. I don't see any other wounds but she might have a head injury. Moira, help me lift her."

As the girls attempted to raise her up, Suki wobbled to her feet on her own.

"Good girl! You'll be alright!" Deirdre said as tears streamed down her face. "Come, let's get you to a vet."

"And let's get you to the station." Garda Dennison yanked on the man who was now in cuffs.

~

The group was still at Shelagh's waiting for the verdict on Suki when Moira and Deirdre returned from the vet. Deirdre reported that Suki's CT scan showed no damage. She had lost a couple teeth and they should watch for swelling, infection or unusual behaviour.

"The gurrier who kicked her should be quartered and boiled in oil! Anyone who would harm an innocent creature deserves the max punishment," Deirdre vehemently declared. "Animals give unconditional, even undeserved love. They ask no questions, make no judgments, never demand an apology, immediately forgive every wrong done to them. There is not a human on the planet that has those qualities. Okay, rant over; but you can see why I sometimes prefer the company of animals to people."

There was a brief moment of silence as everyone absorbed Deirdre's outburst. Then Nuala cleared her throat and said, "As to the sting, we were right. It was that chancer from the dream work group, Brent Nixon. Garda McClellan reported that the two thieves have been cooperative. They provided an address in Cork of a warehouse where their stolen goods are kept. The gardai want Seán to come by next week to identify anything taken from his place."

Seán laughed. "I told them they were welcome to the lot; save me the trouble of an estate sale. I guess I still need to go identify it all, but seriously, I was going to bin most of it anyway. I'd already sold off the wine collection, which was the most valuable. Identification will be easy thanks to Moira's suggestion that we take photographs of the rooms we explored for ghosts in September. Even though no ghostly presence showed up in them, I've got a cracking photographic inventory now."

"And all is well here, Shelagh?" Deirdre asked.

"A couple broken vases in the kerfuffle that ensued when they grabbed the bloke; and of course, the broken window on my back door," Shelagh replied.

"We hear you; We've been through the very same issue not long ago," Moira commiserated.

"We'd better get back to Schull, let Ma know what's going on. I called her earlier but didn't tell her all the details. She'll be worried sick by now wondering about Suki." Nuala looked over at Seán. "You ready?"

"I'm getting used to having a chauffeur; let's go!"

After updating their ma and reassuring her that Suki was fine, the three sisters gathered in Nuala's room. "I'm glad you and Seán worked out your issues and have had this time together here to get to know one another," Deirdre began. "He's a good bloke. You never did tell us, though, when did you first realise you were attracted to him?"

"Oh, that first day we met, at St. Brendan's, when he gave me his arm to lean on as we walked to the rectory. And he is a good lad! He told me he was smitten when I called him to tell him about the Anpost losing his baptismal certificate. My 'passion for his cause' warmed his heart, he said. And do you know? He has actually signed us both up for dance lessons! They don't start until the new year, so by then his cast will be off."

Moira's mobile rang, interrupting their chat. It was Garda Keating from the Dublin Garda Station with an update.

"We struck gold with the third bloke—Martin Harkness. Once we told him we had Susanna in custody, he couldn't talk fast enough. It wasn't his idea, he didn't want to do it, it was an accident, they only meant to scare him, he's very sorry, and plenty more to get them all life sentences."

"Wonderful news! Justice for Denny and clearing his name of suicide will help his mum heal. Were you able to get mobile records? Did they help at all?" Deirdre wanted all the details.

"We did. Enough to establish the initial connection and justify bringing them in for questioning. That way we were able to leave your visitations and dreams out of any official records." They could almost hear the smile in her voice.

"Thank you, Garda Keating, for believing us and getting results. I hope we can work together again sometime," Moira said, wanting to leave the door open for future collaborations.

"Sure, and we will. Oh, and if you ever see my Nana Elinor, tell her I said hiya!"

Gail Grant Park

"May the nourishment of the earth be yours,
May the clarity of light be yours,
May the fluency of the ocean be yours,
May the protection of the ancestors be yours."

—From 'A New Year's Blessing' by John O'Donohue

THE END
—

ATTRIBUTION OF QUOTES

Page 93, "In all of our ancient stories …" Kari Hohne. http://cafeausoul.com Used by permission.

Page 129, "All of us are in danger of dying …" Alan Bradley, from *The Golden Tresses of the Dead*, Delacorte Press, January 2019. Used by permission.

Page 133, "Only in fully releasing the desire for things to be different than they are …" Aine Divine - YouTube, used by permission.

Page 153, "Women are the voices of that Otherworld …." Dr. Sharon Blackie (http://sharonblackie.net) used by permission.

Page 207, "Spectres hovered gloomily over the reedy Marsh …" Donald Ross of the Inverness Gaelic Society as quoted by James Bonwick in his paper entitled, *Irish Druids and Old Irish Religions*, for the Library Ireland (kubraryireland.com)

Page 295, "The Universe puts things in your way ..." Jessica Siemers. Used by permission.

Page 325, "Being human is definitely cumbersome ..." Amanda Lux from 'A Lone Traveler's Guide to the Divine' podcast. Used by permission.

AFTERWORD

Although strictly a work of fiction—all characters are wholly the work of my imagination—many of the names are taken from my Irish ancestry. Thomas and Ellen (Kiely) Connolly were indeed my great-grandparents. Thomas and his brother, Cornelius, did go to the Klondike for several years during the Alaskan Gold Rush. (Alas, they did not return with fortunes).

And although the incidents of visitations from the Otherworld are also fictional, some are based on actual events that either I have experienced, have been told to me by people I know and trust, or are of historic veracity. For those who wish more details on these, and other elements found in this story, you can access them on my website:

https://gailgrantpark.weebly.com/blog/paranormal-experiences-influencing-we-are-shadows/

About the Author

Undeterred after being denied admission to an elite middle school, based (she's sure) on her impromptu short story assignment, Gail continued to write throughout her school years: poetry, journaling, and creative writing. As an adult, she's been an avid blogger, writer of short stories, and biographer to several of her ancestors. Gail is a retired librarian, a genealogist, an herbalist, and grandmother to thirteen amazing grandchildren. She resides in Boise, Idaho, with her husband and their Anatolian Shepherd, Loki.

You can find her at:

https://gailgrantpark.weebly.com

www.Facebook.com/ParkCreativeWriting/

Made in the USA
Columbia, SC
28 August 2024